The Stake in the Game

Books by Evelyn Berckman

The STAKE in the GAME

c. 2

Evelyn Berckman

Doubleday & Company, Inc.
Garden City, New York
1973

ISBN: 0-385-05285-5
Library of Congress Catalog Card Number 72-84889
Copyright © 1973 by Evelyn Berckman
Printed in the United States of America
First Edition

I have to thank Mr. Randolph Whately most gratefully for his help and advice concerning technical legal points in this story.

Au pair: literally, 'on an equality'. Term applied to foreign girls in England filling part-time domestic situations while living with their employers on a family basis and receiving pocket-money, with free hours as individually agreed for purposes of study, etc. There are thousands of au pairs in England, mostly of French, German, Austrian and Spanish nationality.

The Stake in the Game

I

To be hopelessly in love with your husband, who fails to love you in return; a strange fate, thought Mrs. Milland. Or rather, after twenty-five years of marriage she no longer thought it consciously, only felt it; it was the element that contained her, as a globe of water a fish. Now, again in daily unconscious habit as old as her marriage, she glanced at him in such a manner as not to be caught at it, and felt as always the same pang of irresistible pleasure. He *pleased* her, that was all there was to it, and against that argument all other arguments fell to the ground like spent arrows. Absurd that a man's pleasing you should be a consideration so final, yet it was so. His shapely head with its cap of brown hair, smooth and compact, no thin places in it; the charming conciseness of his lips and chin, the refined but masculine modeling of his features, and the ironic intelligence they framed; his excellent body, medium-tall and in perfect proportion, no part of it yet gone thick or sagging—nor would it ever, she could almost believe, as if he had power to impose on his body, as on everything, the quality of control that was his central characteristic. He ate his breakfast composedly, with fastidious detachment; with the same elegance and composure he ordered his daily life, business and social, and slept with his wife. Early in their marriage, when her love for him could only be called agonizing, she would yield herself to the dark abyss of this hunger and longing and fling her arms fiercely about him, wooing him with the urgency of her body and with sounds, formless sounds that had little to do with words, and only with belatedness had felt his distaste and withdrawal.

'My dear,' he had murmured once—only that one time—after some months of her unabating adoration, 'don't be intense.'

And it was enough; with three words in the dark, with the amused embarrassment in those three words, he had shamed and crippled her forever. From now on her love-making was painfully bound with calculation and constraint, and her whole daily behaviour not less so, for fear of offending him. Or fear of amusing him, a thousand times worse; from that lethal amusement of his in their marriage-bed she had never really recovered.

Then, in sequence equally old but inevitable, the rusty needle of self-question fell into another groove: by what lack in herself had she failed in her marriage? By what blindness, stupidity, lack of imagination, had she missed the way to her husband's heart? Her certainty—one of her few certainties—was of the secret core in every nature that can be found and touched; a key to this secret matrix of love existed in Ian, as it existed in everyone else. But there was no question of her ever having had this key and lost it. She had never lost it for she had never found it; another woman, not she, might have been able to find it . . .

The rusty needle, from ancient habit, scraped implacably to the next groove: was there in fact such a woman? Had her husband, in his life, someone to whom he had given what he could never give her? For this thought, which at one time had been a blow in the pit of her stomach and a cold swooning in her head, she now had nothing but a dispassionate scrutiny and assessment. On final balance moreover she always ended by deciding against; his hatred of superfluous exertion and complication, in equal measure, would operate against a secret affair. No, it was highly unlikely that he had, in some innermost fold of his life, an all-releasing passion. And even if he were aware of having missed it, he would not mind. She minded; it was the difference between them. He was in all probability an impeccably faithful husband, for all his constant unspoken derogation of her; perhaps he was even quite fond of her in his way, so she must make do with fondness. It was too late for anything else, anyway. By now she recognized the distance he had created between them as the final link in her subjection; the riveting of her senseless, awful, unbreakable fixity on the unattainable.

By the mind's magic the endless shades and half-shades of all this had passed in an instant, like a light momentarily cast among moveless forms of stagnation in an old well. She was recalled by Ian's asking Paul, 'You're off somewhere this weekend?'

'Yes, Sir,' Paul returned. 'Lyneal.'

He never offered details and his father never asked for them, always appearing satisfied—even pleased—with minimal answers. In the face of their double reticence her own impulse

3

to ask questions, often harassingly anxious, went to the wall as usual. But glancing from Ian to Paul she smiled, as always, the same wry inward smile. The same-shaped head, the same features and voice and intonations; Paul's cap of hair was heavier, superbly brown and burnished where Ian's had gone neutral and was elegantly threaded with grey, but from left to right over each forehead ran an identical ripple, a small breaking wave. There they sat, each one contained in his inviolable capsule of well-mannered reserve; Paul was slightly the taller, his body not yet as compact as the older man's. Otherwise he was a replica of his father, a replica exact to the point of ludicrousness. It was as though, in the very moment of his conception twenty-two years ago, submission was already so planted in her body—its blind and eyeless places as well as its conscious ones—that her drop of albumen enclosing the person to come had utterly capitulated, abdicating from every quality of its own to the beloved invader; at least she had never been able to see any trace of herself, mental or physical, in her son.

What at the moment she *could* see—as if she had never seen it before—was his masculine allure, and the fact that this allure seemed greater from day to day and would go on increasing, presumably, for the next ten years. How attractive to women he must be already, and what an amount of devastation he might cause in his life; had he a girl already, an unofficial fiancée even . . . ? Of details like this she knew absolutely nothing and could deduce nothing from the girls she had seen him with, and inviting his confidence when his father was so pointedly content to let well alone seemed presumptuous, if not foolhardly. Then all at once, with a faint qualm as from the touch of cold metal, she felt his aloof and slightly inhuman quality, Ian's all over again, and wondered

4

if—again like Ian—he would use it to inflict on some unfortunate girl the same sort of withering and pain.

Then she stopped thinking well-worn futilities and sat in a momentary void, a woman of charming looks and appealing grace, but her loveliness veiled—impeded as it were—by her hesitant air, her faint unconscious look of anticipated defeat.

'How long is the run to Lyneal?' Ian was asking.

'I can do it in well under three hours,' Paul returned amicably. 'With good luck I've kept it to two.'

'Fair enough,' Ian nodded. 'Fair enough.' They relapsed into silence with a contented air of no more to be said, this sort of talk being all they ever exchanged, in her hearing at least.

Mrs. Milland however, if she still heard, was not listening. Or rather she was listening intently to an inner voice of her own that—however she tried to silence it for fear of trouble—goaded her more distractingly from day to day. *Ask him, ask him, you fool*, it dinned at her. *The more you put it off, the less you'll have the nerve. Let time slip away, a year here, two years there, and all at once you've gone slack, you've let it go too long, and that's the end. End of you, end of your life, you've amounted to nothing. Ask him, ask him!* the voice clamoured more stridently. *This one thing, it's what you want now more than anything, you've wanted it for years. Ask him—!*

Yet all at once the hateful wavering cancelled her, the habit of uncertainty and of expecting the gentle, mocking rebuff. . . . *Oh God, why am I such a coward?* she mourned. *But I am, I just am, that's all.* But the voice persisted, its imperative accent of command dwindling to the poorer one of question. *Ask him?* it debated weakly. *Or not? Ask him? not ask him?*

The pantry door was pushed inward with unnecessary force and Chantal the au pair, black-haired and stormy-browed, came through and deposited a rack of toast on the table. Her way of putting it down, her way of slapping the door open to come in and slapping it open to go out, had all been part of the same insolence.

Neither of the men had given her so much as a glance; it was Mrs. Milland who sat up straight all at once. Her eyes, suddenly intent and as warlike as it was in them to become, missed nothing of the girl's performance and followed her out of the room. And if within her the erosion and discontent of her unspoken request still lingered, in Chantal's direction she felt nothing but concentrated purpose. She was angry, and ready for battle.

II

The phone call could not have come at a more inconvenient and inopportune moment. With imbecile mechanical insistence it shrilled and shrilled till it brought Mrs. Milland erupting from the kitchen with flushed cheeks and an air of arrested momentum, to snatch it up and challenge rather than answer, 'Hal-*lo!*'

An instant's silence followed before a voice came hesitantly, 'Heather?'

'Oh.' The concentrated irritation of her tone vanished as by magic. 'Sorry, darling, I didn't mean to shout at you.'

'Are you all right?' her sister queried. 'You sounded so funny.'

'No, no, I—I was hurrying, perhaps I sounded a bit blown.'

'Oh.' The monosyllable, unconsciously dismissive, Mrs. Milland recognized for Robina's preliminary to an exposure of her troubles, of which she always had plenty. 'Listen, Heather darling, will you do something for me?'

'Of course.' Already alerted for something worse than usual by the quavering voice, like an untuned string being plucked, Heather's stance at the phone assumed, unconsciously, a new tension. 'What is it?'

'Heather.' Robina could be heard to take breath. 'Are you alone?'

'Yes.'

'You're sure? There's no one at home—?'

'No one at all.'

'But the—the invasion?'

In the sisters' family shorthand *invasion* meant *Gallic invasion*, denoting Heather's current au pair, usually French.

'In the kitchen.' There was no telephone extension in the kitchen. 'Go ahead, darling, it's all right.'

'Heather.' Robina drew another trembling breath. 'Will you say I was with you all this afternoon? Will you, Hezz?'

'Wait, wait,' Heather adjured. Neither caution nor cowardice impelled her lack of immediate consent, only a need—on Robina's behalf, not on hers—to understand the circumstances. Inwardly she could hear little but her own inward clamour of *I must help her, I've got to help her, she's up to her eyebrows —in something worse than usual, by the sound of her.* 'What's it all about?'

'Not now—not like this. But if you'd just say I was with you this afternoon—? will you, Hezz?'

'Of course, darling, of course I will,' she responded fervently, helpless to do otherwise; the sob that answered her, grateful and relieved, wrenched her heart. 'But see here, hadn't you better drop in and enlighten me a bit? give me some idea—?'

'I—I'd better not, not just straightaway, something might be

8

made of it—' the distraction in Robina's voice sharpened; she broke off. 'You're *sure* you're alone?'

'Yes, yes, Robbie—absolutely.'

'Well then. I hate talking about it over the—the—but—Oh hell, it's the usual thing, but this time it turns out that—' she fought the terror in her voice '—Hugh's been having me followed.'

'Oh my God, *no!*'

'Oh my God, yes. The only bright spot is that Basil was in the porter's good graces thank God, the man rang up from downstairs to warn him, and I bundled into my clothes and out the service door just as the—the agent or spy or whatever one calls that sort of vermin, was ringing the doorbell, Oh *God—!*' She was talking so fast and swallowing so often that her meaning now and again was garbled. 'It was horrid, horrid, I was sick with fright. And Basil pale as ashes and ice-cold with disgust—blaming me, he didn't say it but you could see it coming out of every pore in his body. Hating me too, wishing he'd never set eyes on me, that's how it takes a man, damn the whole filthy lot of them. But you see.' She breathed deeply again, a harsh trembling sound. 'I wasn't caught dead to rights, not actually. And so long as there's a doubt, and you back me up—'

'Of course I shall,' Heather reassured. 'Don't worry about that.'

'Thank you, Hezz, Oh thank you.'

Robina's abased voice caught again at Mrs. Milland's heart. *Don't be humble,* silently she entreated her sister, her lovely, unhappy, unlucky sister. *Don't be humble, I can't bear it.* 'We were together from when?' she queried aloud. 'Two-thirtyish till five? Does that cover the times?'

'Oh yes, that's perfect.'

'And what did we do, go shopping, or—?'

'Oh no, let's keep it simple, I mean—if they ask where and when and we come unstuck on details . . . no, I just stopped at home with you, and you were doing a water-colour, and we nattered and had tea. That way there's nothing to come apart at the seams—' she stopped short on a note of panic. 'Oh God, what if the invasion says differently?'

'That one!' Mrs. Milland's laugh was not amused. 'In the house a single moment longer than she can help? No fear. Actually she's just going out now, I stopped her for the purpose of . . . a few words.'

'Well, for God's sake, speed her on her way.'

'I shall,' promised Mrs. Milland grimly, with double-edged meaning. 'I shall.'

'Good.' Relief and concern with her own troubles made Robina deaf to her sister's peculiar tone. 'That's all right then.'

'By the way,' Mrs. Milland reminded sharply, glancing at her wrist. 'It's almost three now. Hadn't we better say you were here from three o'clock on?'

'I reckon. Clever girl, you think of everything.—God, is there any harder work,' she exploded, 'than setting up a lie? And you're such a rotten liar, pet!'

'I know.' Meekly Heather acknowledged her disability. 'But in a case like this, when it's for you, and so frightfully important—I shall be all right. I've got to be all right,' she affirmed stoutly. 'So don't worry, darling, try not to worry.'

'You've saved my life,' Robina quavered. 'I'll try not to give you any more practise at it.' Her voice had turned wry. 'But you can imagine how Hugh's licking his chops and promising himself a field-day, damn his rotten beastly soul, and why do I insult the beasts?'

'Quite.' With Robina's fears allayed, she was prepared in her windblown way to be discursive—*only not now*, thought her elder sister with sudden fatigue and absent-mindedness, *not just at this moment* . . .

'Well, thank you again, darling, from the bottom of my worthless heart. Oh Hezzer, I *wish* I could see you—!'

'Come now,' Heather returned instantly. 'Since you're theoretically here, anyway?'

'Oh no, better not, I mean actually I'd . . . rather not. I can't tell you how shaken I am, somehow I've got to be alone. And I can't even go home because of the servants!' She laughed despairingly. 'I'll find me a cinema and just sit in the dark and sleep till five.'

'Well then, come when you like—whenever you like.'

'Next week,' an unsteady voice promised. 'Soon as I've pulled myself together.—Oh, if I could rub his face in it, that charming husband of mine!' Another voice was speaking— coarse, grating, unrecognizable. 'Let's hope he spends the earth on his rotten agents, and gets damn all out of it!'

On this benediction, having rung off at last, Mrs. Milland stood perfectly still for a moment, dizzied by opposing harassments—her sister's sudden trouble, and what her sister's trouble had interrupted. Then she stood another moment, trying to recover the impetus of attack to which she had wound herself so painfully, and which now was all but lost through the untimely phone-call. But dithering out here was no good, the situation still hung over her head and had to be dealt with, and she would deal with it. With another hesitation, infinitesimal, she walked out of the hall with unnatural rapidity, prepared to plunge once more into the fray.

In the kitchen she found Chantal, in the outrageous dress and cannibal-queen's hair-do she affected for her excursions abroad, exactly where she had left her, as if frozen for all time in her slouching yet defiant stance. Upon her employer's entrance, except for the expressionless look she threw from dark sombre eyes, darker still under her thatch of dark heavy hair, no part of her moved.

'Well, Chantal,' Heather resumed, with a dismaying sense of scattered momentum. The angry courage she had felt at breakfast, then lost during hours of soft-hearted dithering and cowardice, then regained during other hours of working herself up to the point of confrontation—to all of it the phone call had been fatal.

'*Mais madame!*' Chantal interrupted dramatically. She abandoned the wall against which she had been leaning slightly, and waved her arms. 'Waat 'ave I don?' Her accent was very strong and her English annoyingly unimproved for the time she had been in the country—a time by no means limited to her sojourn with the Millands. And even if by repute the French were poor linguists, with this girl Heather put it down to pure laziness.

'If you please tell me,' she was pursuing in a throbbing Gallic voice, 'waat 'ave I—'

'Oh Lord! I've told you.' Heather welcomed the spur of anger, lost and now resurrected. 'There's not one single thing you're supposed to do here, that you do decently or even half-decently. You're neglectful and slovenly, you walk out of here the moment you can and come back at all hours. After all, the obligations aren't *entirely* on our side, you've got some too, and the way you simply ignore them—'

'Oh please, madame, more slow—'

'—you *use* this house, that's all, you simply—'

'Please, please,' Chantal besought again. 'Oo-enn you talk so fass I do not onnerstan'—'

'*Cette maison, pour vous, ce n'est qu'une convenance,*' Heather plunged into a language over which she had little more than a school-room command. '*Uniquement une convenance, c'est tout! Il n'y a pas un seul de vos devoirs que vous achevez bien, ou consciencieusement—*'

'Bot—bot som times,' Chantal put in, for some reason in English, 'som times you 'ave tell me somssing, and per'aps I do it bad because I do not onnerstan'—'

'I've always explained very clearly and slowly.' *Cunning*, Heather seethed inwardly, *low cunning*. 'Anyway, your work here is so simple that even a fool could hardly misunderstand. And you're no fool, Chantal.'

'Vous allez donc me jeter dehors, you weel put me out?' quavered Chantal bilingually on a high note of incredulity and anguish. 'Bot oo-aire shall I go?' She flung her arms out again. 'Oo-aire shall I go?'

'Where you go is no concern of mine,' retorted Heather. Again a welcome hardness invigorated her at the demand and the pathos, so flagrantly false. 'You were living in London before you came to us, you told me so yourself. So go back to where you were, or do exactly as you please.' She permitted herself a moment of unaccustomed malice. 'Judging by your comings and goings, I should say you knew your way about pretty well, by this time.'

She paused all at once or rather checked, for no more reason

13

than the new look in Chantal's eyes; to naked hatred from any source, few are impervious.

'I'll pay you for this month, and for an extra month,' she resumed, throwing off as well as she could the impact of that black, burning look; it had shaken her considerably. 'I want to be fair. Heaven knows why, you've been anything but fair to us. I'll give you till Saturday afternoon to find somewhere to live, that's almost three days. Don't bother about the house any more, it can hardly make any difference. So that's that,' she said conclusively. 'Please be out by Saturday afternoon, I don't care how or where, but be *out*. Not another word,' she cut across Chantal's opening mouth. 'I don't want to hear any more about it. I've given you chance after chance, I've told you and told you you'd have to do better, and I might as well have talked to a post.'

Having to pause for breath, she realized she was going at such a rate that the girl must have lost the half of what she was saying; also she had determined to be quiet but firm, and resentfully heard her voice ascending to a virago's. 'Now that's enough, nothing you say can make any difference, it's too late.—You were just going out, I believe?' she asked with polite and deliberate irony. 'Don't let me detain you further, Chantal.'

III

Robina allowed an interval of five days, turning up on Tuesday; at once her mood could be seen as chancy.

'Go on working,' she commanded her sister irritably, after they had come upstairs. 'Go on, Hezz, it—it steadies me to watch you. I want to be quiet a moment—have a puff and pull myself together.'

A pause fell between them, seated in the curious enclosure derisively known as 'The Studio'—no more than a bubble stuck on the rear wall of the first-floor living-room overlooking the garden; in other days one of those miniature glass-houses for lady horticulturists, but forlorn and derelict when they had bought the house, cobweb-clotted and with panes missing or broken. Its demolishment, instantly decreed by Ian, was as instantly opposed by Heather's urgent request to have it for her own use, and Ian had agreed with entire good humour and a genial, 'Quite good enough for dabbling.' His wife, accepting without demur this definition of her talent, seized upon the minute eyrie, and for the last ten years this domain—

about seven feet by seven—had been her refuge and her escape, the sole place in which she could feel a positive happiness. Weathertight now, painted and repaired and trim, its front glass left clear and the sides and roof whitewashed, its combined transparency and translucency afforded inexhaustible effects of sun, cloud, and rain. Here Heather sat with her brushes and colours and pursued the secrets of light: anomalies of dulled light and bright shadow, flying gleams bright or dark, strangeness of overcast that turned everything cold and leaden or thick brooding sulphur-colour; the same objects became quite different objects under alteration of light. She painted light-splintered petals of flowers, the spiked wall at the garden's far end that menaced so dramatically on a gloomy day; sometimes she made a picture circumscribed by a single pane, sometimes let two or three panes cut a picture into as many asymmetric sections. She attempted anything and everything provided she thought she could handle it, things she considered small subjects; her estimate of her abilities, always modest, was more and more derogatory.

Continuing to work as ordered, she glanced furtively once or twice at her sister, smoking and staring into some comfortless beyond, and with familiar resigned apprehension waited for her to speak. Yet in her anxiety she thought how lovely Robina was, even with her present look—harassed and petulant—that would spoil any face but the prettiest. Under this hard unsparing daylight she had no lines but what a girl of twenty-five might have; how charming her short straight nose, her blunt sensual lips and round chin. More russet in colouring than auburn, she had the creamy skin that goes with the type, and her soft heavy fox-coloured hair had the disciplined swirl and lustre provided by the ministrations of London's

16

most expensive hair-dressers twice a week. In this durable beauty, all that ever changed were her eyes; unhappiness or worry, dislike or bad temper, turned their bright amber to an opaque brown almost ugly, and seemed to decrease their size. At the moment they showed this muddy thickening, a portent —Heather thought indistinctly—of nothing good to come.

'Well.' Abruptly Robina jettisoned her cigarette and re-settled on the kitchen chair; the tiny space barely contained two people. 'Well, I don't know if I've anything to tell you, good or bad.' She paused to light up again and take a short exasperated puff. 'Nothing's happened actually, since I rang you.' She drew on her cigarette, her lips retracting in a grimace that showed her teeth. 'But that day, I mean that evening, Hugh's expression—you should have seen it. Let-down, you know, *disappointed!* It was so indecently transparent, I almost laughed in his face.'

She laughed now, a glittering icicle of sound.

'Tantalizing, you know, because I was seen to go into the building, undeniably I was *seen*, but that's all of it. He had me, but not quite—so near and yet so far.' The savagery of her laugh, this time, broke midway and fell into some fear-haunted rift. 'All the same it's—it's not nice, you know. I find him watching me with those—those hateful eyes of his, *mean,* you've noticed his eyes? Oh Hezz, suppose after all he . . . he knows something. Suppose there's something he's—he's found out—'

'What?' Heather demanded forcibly. 'Unless you're keeping something back—'

'I'm not, I'm not!'

'Well then, he can't have found out anything—or not about that particular day.'

'How do I know that? How do *you* know? You can't be sure. He knows something, of course he does. He must, he—'

'Look.' Heather countered the accent of rising hysteria. 'Could anyone have been listening at your end, when you spoke to me?'

'How could they? I rang from a hotel.'

'Well then.'

'Your house wasn't empty,' Robina snuffled, with patent disbelief in her own suggestion.

'Rot! Chantal was in the kitchen, I told you. And even if she'd been glued to an extension,' Heather pursued sardonically, 'you were safer than ever. Her English is basic, and that's overdoing it. She's never once taken a message over the phone and got it right, not once, and if you speak fast she's completely lost. And you, my love, were going nineteen to the dozen, that day—I lost you once or twice, myself.'

'You can say that.' Robina was shivering visibly. 'It's easy for a bystander. M-my God, this waiting to see what he'll do, this w-w-*waiting!* I'll go mad, I'll start climbing the wall, I'll—'

'Shut up,' Heather silenced the frenzied whimper. 'Shut up a moment and let me think.'

In a following total silence she embarked on that most difficult of all exercises, putting one's self—really putting one's self—in the other person's place.

'I think, myself, that Hugh's in a difficult position.' Her strenuous thinking had provided her with qualifications, if not conclusions. 'The whole point is, has he asked you anything directly—about where you were that afternoon?'

'N-no.'

'There you are, you see, I was sure of it—he's in a cleft stick. He can hardly question you point-blank without giving the game away. And supposing he did ask you and you told him what we've rigged—well, on my end, I hardly see him turning up on our doorstep to put me through any inquisition. He won't, anyway,' she added with sudden divination. 'He'll know we've had time to arrange our lie in advance. He'll take it for granted we're ready, he's no fool.'

She frowned with the effort of negotiating this pitted terrain, so utterly foreign and difficult through her deplorable lack of deviousness; aware only of her sister's foundering wits in the face of imminent shipwreck, and knowing only that she must think for her sister. 'So that's it, darling, that's how I see it. My guess is he'll cut his losses this time, he'll know he hasn't enough to go on. He'll just drop this particular thing, you won't hear any more about it.' She drew a long breath; her eyes withdrew from straining after unknown shapes in some future murk, and returned to Robina. 'But he'll try again, you know, and it's up to you to give him nothing to find. He'll wait and he'll watch. Well, let him watch—till his eyes drop out.'

'Amen,' Robina reciprocated cordially, and veered—in her erratic way—from overdone misgiving to ill-advised triumph. 'Thank you for straightening me out, darling, I was much too shattered to think. Anyway—' her spirits rose, visibly, another degree '—that block of flats is so big one might easily know more than one person who lived there, just seeing me go in won't give little Hughie chapter and verse for his divorce. So,' she jeered, 'what'll he do next?'

'Next? for divorce?' The word seemed to return her, if not her giddy sister, to the brink of still other unknown chasms. 'I expect it'll all depend on how much he wants it. Just how anxious is he, would you say—for divorce?'

A silence followed, not long but of peculiar depth, intensifying her vision of earth-rents opening silently at their feet.

'I don't know.' Robina's tone, objective, indicated at least a momentary composure. 'It's not simple. With anyone but my charming husband, I might have some idea. But with Hugh, damn and blast his scabby soul, I don't expect he's anxious just for divorce, it wouldn't satisfy him. Cruel, you know, he's so beastly cruel he'd be more anxious to *punish*—get back at everyone involved, make as much hell for them as possible. First and foremost he'd try to destroy the man—with bad publicity, sue him for damages, ruin him with legal costs, those things alone would finish most people. Then when he'd got back at the man—then and not till then—he'd turn his attention to me.'

She paused in assessment and conjecture.

'I'm not even sure he'd divorce me,' she pursued sombrely. 'He might and he might not, according to which he thought would be hardest for me. If he could sling me out with every conceivable humiliation and make sure I hadn't a bean to live on, yes, that he'd do. But if he suspected that divorce would let me escape—into a chance of being happy with someone else—no, he'd never let me go, never. He'd see me dead first.'

Thoughtfully she drew on her cigarette.

'So that's as far as I can see into dear Hughie,' she pursued. 'He's a dark horse as well as a bloody bastard. But one thing I *am* sure of—anyone that goes up against him is lost. Because he's so rotten rich that . . . that every advantage on earth—he's got it, or he can buy it . . .'

Her voice faded; her eyes, bleak, canvassed no future.

'But you—you yourself,' Heather essayed, after the pause. Her sister's frozen look, whether of composure or petrified ex-

haustion, alarmed her. 'Darling, if he did divorce you, it might
be the best thing. You might meet someone else, or find some
work—'

'Don't be a nit,' Robina interrupted savagely. 'Why should
I count on finding someone now, if I couldn't when I was
twice as good-looking? Men—God, how I *hate* them! Use you
and run like hell at the least hint of trouble . . . And work?
what work? wash dishes in a caff? stand behind a counter at
Woolworth's? I've my looks because I can afford to take care
of them. How long would they last in some squalid little job?
How long would *I* last? I'd be a hag in no time, an old ugly—'

'Robbie—' Heather attempted.

'—anyway I'm not well, I'm never well, it's the strain of
being always unhappy—'

'But anything,' Heather put in. 'Anything might be better
than the rotten life you're leading—'

'Rotten,' the other bore her down loudly, 'but dashed comfortable. And don't be an utter quixotic fool, you've always
been.'

'All right, all right,' surrendered the elder, unconditionally.
'Shut up a moment, will you? Now look.' Her whole longing,
intense to painfulness, was to buttress this crumbling struc-
ture, so lovely, so useless; buttress it with love and keep it
from falling apart. Robina's beauty and elegance seemed to
her all at once the most pitiful of defenses, flimsy and pathetic. 'You weren't caught this time, it's all that matters. And
now you know he's trying to trap you and you simply don't
give him another chance, that's all.'

'And a lot of fun that sounds, in a pig's eye.' Robina
veered abruptly from tragedy to aggressive discontent. 'Invisible chastity-belt.'

'It means you must be careful for awhile,' Heather gain-said. 'It doesn't mean taking vows.'

'Stop laughing at me, you bitch. Darling Hezzer.' Mispro-nounced names and nicknames, bits of their childhood, still floated in their lives. 'But you don't know, Sweetie, you don't live in the same house with a man who's physically repulsive to you. If he touched me, if he so much as touched me—' her face was unrecognizable for an instant '—I'd claw his eyes out. Anyway he's never been worth a damn in bed, I've noticed that very big tall men often aren't.' With the uninhibited practicality of a carpenter discussing measurements, Robbie was given to discussing such phenomena. 'A nice compact gent, medium-sized, has it all over these big loosely-put-together—' with typical inconsequence she interrupted herself as her restless eyes found a new focus; she leaned forward. 'I say, that's jolly good, what you're doing.' She stared at the emerging water-colour. 'That's really lovely. Oh Hezzer, you lucky thing with something to *do*—!'

The cry of envy and despair seemed to hang in the air be-tween them; Heather's face, curiously blank all at once, re-vealed no more than her steady hands that guided her brushes in their changeless orbit of colour, water, paper; colour, water, paper. . . .

'I don't know,' she said, after the pause.

'What do you mean you don't know, you ungrateful wench?'

'I don't seem to be getting any forwarder.' The casualness of her murmur disclaimed her weariness of heart. 'It's not much fun to feel that you're . . . you're merely treading water.'

'Well, of course!' Robina's face was different, all alive with comprehension. 'I understand exactly—you're in a rut. You've gone as far as you can on your own, and now you've come up against a blank wall. What you need now is help, a year or two of really tough professional instruction—people to open new doors for you.'

'How—' Heather's voice, after a moment, was almost soundless. '—how did you know?'

'Well, I must say!' Robina bridled in exaggerated burlesque. 'I'm not *entirely* a clod, I may be a whore but I'm not a stupid whore. Long ago I was supposed to have a few talents, and I did, didn't I?' Suddenly the question was a naked, anguished plea. 'I was good at music and dancing and drawing, Hezzer, wasn't I?'

'You were better than I ever was,' Heather returned. 'At everything.'

'I don't say that.' Consoled patently if inexplicably, she returned to the attack. 'But I haven't *always* lived in outer darkness, you know. Heather, for Christ's sake.' She leaned forward again; her turbid eyes cleared and warmed to a beautiful golden brown, her voice became fervent. 'Why don't you go at this seriously, darling? Why don't you *do* something about it?'

'I want to,' Heather admitted neutrally. 'I've been dying to, for a long time.'

'Well then, you fool—?'

The small silence was large enough to contain the implication; with no need of telling, Robina's intuitions leaped on it like a tigress. 'Ian? But why would he object? why would he possibly object?'

'What I'd like to do,' Heather enunciated carefully; strange to hear her secret longing, for the first time, in words. '—what I'd like to do actually is go to a man in Paris, Dubost, and work in his studio—he's marvelous, I know he's exactly what I need. Six months at least, less than that's no good, and a year's better. If you knew how I want to . . .' her voice expired.

'Well.' Robina took her up smartly. 'Talk to Ian about it then. Why don't you, Heather? why *don't* you?'

'Actually, I . . . I'm going to.' The sound of her voice, surprising her, simultaneously inspired her with no conviction at all. 'I've been working up courage for a long time, and I'm more or less at the point. Why not, why not?' she demanded. 'Why shouldn't I?'

'Why shouldn't you, indeed.'

'It's not as though they needed me.' Heather, unhearing in her turn, yielded herself to exhorting soliloquy. 'They need me for absolutely nothing. Paul's a young man with a life of his own—of which, by the way, I know next to nothing. And Ian—in his mind I'm something connected with a smoothly-running house and his daily comfort, but no more than that, I'm sure of it. They're both so—so inhumanly self-sufficient,' she strove on. 'They—they somehow—I don't mean they're actually against me,' she explained inexactly. 'But if there were a real difference of opinion I feel that they—they'd close ranks, stand together, I'd be the outsider. They make me feel like that now—shut out.'

'Smug bastards. And all the more reason for you to get cracking on this, you've no time to waste.' Robina's voice was peremptory. 'Tell Ian what you're going to do and make your arrangements to study with this French bloke, and go *to* it. If you don't now, when will you? Life's not forever.' Her urgency was more and more pressing. 'You're forty-six. Put it off another few years, you'll be indifferent, you won't want things any more.—Why, that's it!' Surprised, she was regarding some discovery of definition. 'Hope's the ability to want. That's it, the mainspring, having the power to want. When you've lost that, you've lost the lot. So promise me?' she demanded, her eyes golden spears of impalement. 'Promise me you'll tell Ian—?'

'Yes,' Heather returned in a pale voice. With cooling ardour she felt the phrase, *Tell Ian,* as a fatal mistake. 'Yes, yes, I'll . . . I'll ask him.'

'Ask him?' Robina, preternaturally alert all at once, regarded her sister with suspicion. 'And if he says no—?'

'Well then, I—I couldn't.'

'You'd give it *up?* just like that?'

'I—yes, I'm afraid I should.'

'You worm,' said Robina. 'You utter, despicable, crawling worm.'

'I can't help it,' Heather strove against her scorn. 'I couldn't go absolutely counter to him in anything important, I couldn't. I mean . . . when you love someone . . . it weakens you, where your own wishes are concerned. Or even if—if love is over, I mean the first tremendous part—it's taken root in you. The habit, I mean, of considering . . . of *wanting* to consider . . . the other person first. Because it's become the —the natural thing to do—'

'The more cowardly thing,' Robina interjected contemptuously. 'You're afraid of him, that's all.'

'Not afr—not afraid exactly.' Honest to the point of life-long embroilment, Heather refined her denial. 'Say I'm afraid of what might happen if I simply ignored Ian and went my own way. Like . . . like . . . Oh damn, I can't explain it,' she admitted. 'It's got nothing to do with thought, only with feeling.'

'When you're submissive like this, you make me want to vomit,' Robina informed her explicitly. 'You're just cowed, that's all.'

Enslaved, thought Heather. *Different from being cowed.* She shrugged slightly with no resentment, only with resignation mirrored in the listless movements of her brush.

'What rotten luck we've had with our men,' Robina offered, after a pause. 'The three of us.'

'The three—?'

'Mummy, you and I. Papa, what a blight! That sour self-righteousness and Olympian gloom—how he could take the life out of anything, don't you remember? And of course Mummy couldn't begin to cope with his ghastly atmosphere, poor gay little sweet. My God, I only hope she had consolation somewhere along the line!' An idea took hold of her visibly and made her sit up straighter. 'Heather, you and I—d'you expect we had the same father?'

'Gracious,' Heather responded mildly. 'If so, it's late in the day to begin worrying about it.'

'Why's worrying? I'd hail the idea of being Mummy's bastard with loud cheers. *You'd* be the legitimate one, the elder—anyway you've got Papa's forehead and eyes, sort of. But look at us.' She scanned the pure oval of her sister's face, the fair skin and classical lips, the pale-brown hair feathered with grey at the temples, the gentleness in which there was nothing tame nor insipid. 'We simply couldn't be more different, could we now? The shape of our heads alone, we've not a bone alike. And our colouring. And our build, you're so *chien de race* and I'm a pit-pony. Darling, you *are* lovely!' she announced with conviction. 'You're still sweet and lovely. And

26

I'm pretty good too, aren't I? I'm still a bedworthy wench—?'

'By all the evidence.' Heather's glance combined irony and tribute; Robina was exquisitely turned out as always in a fascinating silky tweed, palpably hand-loomed and a limited edition. Its subtle tawny heightened her own russet colouring; at her throat she wore a gold collar of thick irregular links, with a matching bracelet on one wrist. 'You're even a little more smashing today than usual.'

'I think so too. Then why's it been no use?' Robina demanded with sudden rancour. 'Our looks, what good've they done us?'

No response came but a movement between Heather's brows, the faintest shadow that might be either perplexity or pain.

'Now *I* married for money,' the other pursued, not pausing for an answer. 'I wanted to marry a rich man and I did, without loving him, so I've asked for what I got and serve me right. But *you*,' she accused, 'you married for love. You were so besottedly in love you were exactly like a—a half-stunned rabbit. And you haven't come off all that well, either.'

Heather's silence, noncommittal, changed imperceptibly to careful.

'Now I'm afraid of Hugh because he's a big hulking brute with a contemptible nature and a filthy temper,' Robina pursued. 'But you're every bit as afraid of Ian, who's an absolute gentleman. So why, *why?* what's it all about, why is it that nothing makes sense—'

Abruptly she stopped; the look and tone of soliloquy fell away from her. 'For Christ's sake, what am I nattering about?' she demanded, and stood up abruptly. 'I'm off. Don't bother to come down with me, Hezz.'

27

'I'd like to.' Heather rose. 'Stretch my legs a bit.'

Yet Robina, having announced her departure, stood stock-still; about her was a sudden wretchedness, a collapse of misgiving.

'Oh Hezz,' she half-whispered. Her colour had turned ghastly, her voice and lips trembled. 'Oh God, I hope I haven't involved you in any mess of my own.'

'What mess?' Her sceptical and repudiating tone belied the contagion of fear in her, the causeless momentary chill. 'In what can you have involved me?'

'I—I don't know, I don't know. But what if something goes wrong, s-s-something. . . .'

'What? It's all between the two of us, entirely. What can go wrong?'

'I—d-d-don't know, I . . .' Robina's teeth chattered, her voice spiraled up to shrillness. 'Oh my God, if I've done you some frightful . . . sort of harm I'll . . . I'll kill myself, I'll—'

'Rot!' Forcibly she reassembled herself to cope with this new crisis. 'Now Robbie, look: what can go wrong? A complicated lie I mightn't manage, but this is so *simple!* We were here together most of Thursday afternoon, period.' Alarmed, she canvassed the disintegration before her, the distressing dampness broken out on forehead and chin. 'Come on, buck up. Come on, Robbie, come *on!'*

Her exhortation took effect; with relief she saw the mask of terror fade and her sister emerge. After a moment Robina, with a grimace of self-disgust and a snowflake handkerchief, began mopping away the shine of panic.

'Thank you,' she offered with a husky voice and an uncertain smile. 'I was going to bits, you know. Thank you again.'

'Oh, shut up. But promise me one thing: be careful. Don't precipitate anything, don't start anything, just wait and see. After all, he can't have you followed forever.'

'Oh, can't he?' Contradiction turned Robina incandescently alive. 'I tell you you don't know our Hughie, it's a knowledge reserved for his lucky little wife.' Her voice was corrosive. 'Where it's a question of a grudge to pay back, he'll never let go, never. He'll wait and wait till he can strike, time makes no difference—a grudge is his dearest possession.' Her ugly laugh matched the ugliness in her face. 'He nurses it and whispers sweet nothings to it, I shouldn't wonder. And when he's hurt someone enough he'll gloat and gloat, he hasn't even the decency to hide it, he—'

'All the same, darling,' Heather put in against the current. 'Don't go all windy, you know I'll stand by you whatever happens. But do be just a little bit—careful, sensible—promise me.'

'I promise.' As by magic, again, Robina was buoyant; a moody creature fleeting from dark to light, like the sky above the glass studio. 'And *you* damned well promise *me* that you'll tackle Ian about studying in Paris. And none of this week-kneed asking him, tell him—just announce it as an accomplished fact.'

'Yes, yes,' Heather evaded. 'I told you I would.'

'Well, *do* it! Promise me?'

'I promise, darling. I do promise.'

IV

Even sitting alone and presumably unobserved, Paul's elegance continued impeccable; with one foot on his knee, his leg canted outward at an angle, he was negligent but gracefully negligent; he never slumped nor sprawled. But the darkness of his face, his air of brooding on some irritation, were rare and uncharacteristic enough to check her slightly the moment she stepped into the living-room. His expression changed at once, however; he rose as promptly for his mother as for a visitor, smiling and saying, 'Hallo, Mummy.'

'Hallo, my love.' In her world so often void of comfort, it was a disproportionate comfort that he had, at least, beautiful manners. And by the contemporary standards of his generation he might have been scruffy, dirty, unshaven and lazy, and he was none of these things. His hair was worn somewhat longer than it would have been worn a few years ago, and his luxuriant sideburns had shrunk before Ian's ironic glance and pointed lack of comment to mere stubs, beautifully barbered; otherwise he was always—formally or informally—well-groomed and well-dressed. But suppose he had chosen to be one of those whiskered youths, a shameless ill-smelling layabout, could Ian—even Ian—have breasted the current trend with any success? She knew fathers far more aggressive than Ian who had fought it out with their sons and lost; the son left home or the father threw him out, or capitulated. The first two procedures were too drastic to recommend themselves to many, while the third must poison a household with the perpetual silent conflict between fatherly disgust and filial defiance. . . .

'Sherry?' he asked as she sat down.

'I shouldn't mind.' Her lingering smile deepened as she admired him; he was extremely handsome in black tie, bound as usual for some party later in the evening. A charmer, that was all there was to it, he charmed without self-consciousness or effort. 'Thank you very much, Paul.' She took a sip or two, having to think as always how she could initiate conversation with him; she had to make talk as if her son were a stranger, and by God she would make it, at the same time avoiding the intrusive nuance of intimacy. 'Actually, have I interrupted a session of heavy thinking? I'll go away, if so.'

'Oh Lord! rather not.' He smiled again and she knew she was beaming, and hoped the overspill of love was not patent enough to irritate him and make him dry up. Evidently not, for he was pursuing, 'The brow was furrowed, you mean? Not all that furrowed actually, I was just mulling—over the inconveniences of friendship.'

'Inconveniences,' she echoed without inquiry.

'Yes, here's someone I know getting married, Bill Jarrold, someone you've never met I expect, he's not even a particular friend of mine—just one of a crowd I happen to see all the time, unfortunately. You know how it is—just because you meet frequently they begin looking on you as closer than a brother, when actually you're no more than an acquaintance.'

'Oh yes,' Heather concurred. Her tone achieved, by carefulest balance, just the right amount of interest; not hungry enough to put him off. 'I know how it happens.'

'Well, blast! there you are. The silly clot had to rope me in as best man.' With a sudden gesture he disordered his smooth burnished hair; at once this ruffled look gave him a charm over and above his well-groomed charm, and made him younger. 'Which means a pretty decent present, and just at the moment when I'm hoarding every copper for my holiday.'

'Well,' she returned. 'It doesn't sound too desperate. An extra fifty pounds?—' Had she offered it too eagerly, with an eagerness he might find displeasing . . . ? 'Would that make things any easier?' she went on perforce, above her misgiving.

'Oh Lord, *no!*' He was genuinely horrified. 'I didn't mention it for that, Mummy.'

'Oh I know, but—'

'It's simply,' he bore on heatedly, 'that one resents being hooked into other people's messes, that's all.'

'Messes . . . ?'

'That's what I call it—when a chap's being dragged up the aisle, for no better reason than the bride's being two months gone.'

'Oh.'

'Exactly—cathedral, bishop, full choir, reception at the Ritz, the lot—for nothing more than a shotgun wedding. Why've *I* got to spend money on this . . . nuptial chain-gang? What respect can I possibly have for the whole bloody show?'

She had never seen him so heated and aggrieved for years,

or at least not so openly. Within her was a shamefaced admission; she was enjoying all of it as a novel treat, and longed for it to go on and on, this sort of talk so many miles removed from the pattern imposed by Ian.

'I haven't the least sympathy for Bill,' he was continuing, carried along by absorption in his topic; now she recognized his discursiveness only as the need to blow off steam, not as confidence reposed in her, and who cared—? 'I know he doesn't love her, early on he even put it about that she wasn't much good in bed. As for the girl, I've more or less disliked her, always. She's just a stupid little nit, but her family are well enough off to make things hell for Bill, quietly—black him professionally, by underground channels—there're ways. He's articled to a solicitor, so they've got him where it hurts— he couldn't be more vulnerable, poor sod.'

'Mmmm.' She barely ventured the syllable, for fear of breaking the thread.

'So there you are—a wedding with the bridegroom bull-dozed into it, or blackmailed. I plump for number two, myself.' His tone was judicial and complacent. 'He looked the probabilities in the face, got scared stiff, and decided he'd settle for *her* face—on the pillow next his, for X years, God help him. Well, that's that.'

'They'll probably divorce later on,' Heather suggested. 'It sounds like it, anway.'

'Divorce,' her son informed her lordlily, 'is no trifle either. It can be dragged out and made damned expensive, and her people will see to it that it is. I saw them at the cocktail party when the engagement was announced—the father, Yorkshire, brrr!' He shuddered dramatically. 'I understand he's livid over the whole thing too, he's got it in for the seducer. If Bill tries to break loose, my guess is he'll cripple him one way or another. No, no, if you ask me poor old Bill's had it—'

He checked all at once and turned on his mother an acknowledging smile that ran all through her like warmth; an instant of radiant happiness to be prized, coming from this undemonstrative young man in his semi-formal elegance.

'Sorry,' Paul was apologizing. 'Sorry to bore you with all this.'

Bore me! her heart echoed, an outcry of protest. *It's a chance to hear about you, you. You're almost all I have and what do I know of how you live or what you do. . . .*

Cool and dispassionate, she said aloud, 'It's an old story, but always a new terrible one, I expect—for the girl. I mean, she's got to be considered too, hasn't she? It can't be pleasant for the girl, ever.'

'Oh Lord, Mummy,' he sighed. 'Don't niff of camphor-balls. A girl not knowing how to take care of herself in this day and age? With clinics and whatnot panting to tell her? Everything's laid on from the first poke to the abortion, the free delivery, the adoption—she can have her choice. Or,' he mocked, 'haven't you heard of the Welfare State?'

'Now and again,' she murmured. 'Vaguely.'

'So if she's caught, she's half-witted. Or unlucky,' he conceded reasonably. 'There *is* such a thing as bad luck.'

'Have you ever thought what you'd do?' Too daring, the question? a liberty in bad taste? She ventured it out of her fascination with these glimpses, so rarely accorded, through a door so rarely opened. 'In a case like that?'

'Do?' Faced with the concrete inquiry (unexpected, she was

34

glad to see) he appeared to readjust his aplomb about him. 'A good question,' he conceded. 'Let me think.'

With pleasure slightly malicious, she suppressed a smile.

'Yes, a damned good question, now you put it to me,' he repeated. 'Let me think it out.'

Respectfully silent, she waited.

'Well,' he said, after cogitation. 'Well, the first thing I'd do would be to ask her how long she'd known about her condition. A lot would depend on her answer, the hell of a lot. If she were one of these irregular totties—lots of them are, you know, from dope and too much sleeping-about, general self-neglect—well, it might actually be that she'd miss and think nothing of it. No, I'd never be hard on the girl for bad luck or honest accident.'

'Would you believe her?' she hazarded. 'How do you know enough of this—this particular cycle—of your girl's?'

'But a chap would know.' His tone was surprised but very gentle, as if explaining to a mental defective. 'If he'd been sleeping with her, naturally he'd know.'

'Oh,' she murmured, an abysmal and embarrassed idiot who hoped she was not blushing. 'In that case then, you'd not blame her?'

'Now wait, wait, I might blame her, in fact I'd be dashed annoyed, but I'd never chuck her. And now,' he reflected, 'now we come to the . . . ah . . . contributing circumstances. With a poor girl, she can't raise all that much stink, no one cares enough. So I say to her, "See here, I'll take care of you as best I can, I'll work it out with my solicitor and you'll be protected." An awful bind, financially,' he observed. 'Damnable hard cheese, but it's right that one should pay for being an ass. It's fair.'

He paused again, and again warring attitudes divided her. His cold-blooded calculation she felt as appalling, yet her passionate interest in this undiscovered entity, her son, impeded her thriving growth of disagreements.

'On the other hand,' he was saying, 'if the girl's people are rich—'

'Yes?' she prompted, ignobly riveted.

'—well, if her family tried to bully me into marriage I simply say, "I'll resist legally, and if you want that sort of stink for your daughter's reputation it's up to you, chums." So then, obviously, they're more interested in hushing it up than I am. Which makes the rich-girl problem, compared with the poor-girl problem,' he concluded masterfully, 'merely a piece of cake.'

'I see,' she murmured, pole-axed.

'Then there's the final possibility—that the girl's let herself get pregnant as a calculated manoeuvre.' His voice hardened. 'To force the bloke into marriage. Oldest man-trap in existence, but Bill's case proves that it still works. Well, let a girl try that with me.' His eyes and youthful jaw became flint. 'Let her try it on, that's all—she'll have had it. Tactics like that, she's released me from everything. From responsibility—from any feeling I'd ever had for her—the lot.'

His vengeful look, pitiless; did it originate, she wondered fleetingly, in some experience of his own . . . ?

'So I simply tell her, "Get your maintenance order and to hell with you—you'll get damned little, it's my father that has money, not I, and you've lost what might have been a friend." So from then on I don't give a tinker's curse what becomes of her, and she's only herself to blame.'

He had passed sentence, obviously, delivered final judgment; again she sat stunned, then rallied enough to offer with faint mockery, 'So there you are, with everything arranged for —everything thought out.'

'Rather.' He was complacent but tried to conceal it; this she found rather sweet of him. 'Might as well know where you're going as not know, h'm?'

'I wish we'd had the recipe in my day.' She was dreamy, perceiving that he suspected no irony. 'The formula.'

'Naturally you wish, who wouldn't?' He conceded, genial. 'But your generation just sat and let things happen to it, whereas mine's got a long way past that sort of nonsense. You were just out of luck, poor old Mummy.'

She paused another moment before delivering her final shot; by no means formidable, he would dispose of it as he disposed of everything. All the same, overwhelmingly curious, she persisted, 'But Paul—what if the girl loved you?'

His sudden silence gave her a rather mean amusement; pleasant to short-circuit that large omniscience, even briefly. 'If love enters into the situation,' she pressed her small advantage, 'what then?'

All in one moment there had flashed across his face the most varying shades of expression, almost too rapid to follow or define: a defensive irritation and stiffening, barriers going up—yet all this prohibitive withdrawal subsiding to the clarity of a reasonable look; he was prepared to acknowledge love as an element to be reckoned with. Along with acquiescence as yet unspoken, he presented the unheard-of spectacle of a flaw in his aplomb. Through her encasing irony, this faint sheepishness weakened her with illogical adoration. Meanwhile she was repeating like a parrot, 'What about love?'

'Love?' Recovering promptly, he answered promptly. 'On both sides, of course, there'd be no problem. You mean love on the girl's part only? one-sided love?'

'Even one-sided love,' she agreed. 'Yes.'

'Do you know the answer?' he returned. His voice was different again, teasing and amused, and a dullness fell over her like a dimming of light. *Now he'll simply slide out of it,* she thought. *Get away from anything he doesn't like by pretending it isn't there, just like Ian.*

'No, I don't know the answer,' she responded lifelessly, relegated to a familiar loneliness. *He'll end it with a clever nothing, a well-bred joke.* Her son, however, disappointed her agreeably; his superior smile had faded and was replaced again by the serious look that became him with such devastating effect.

'I agree with you,' he said. 'It's something one would have to consider. Well, if the girl loved me—and if I simply didn't want to marry her—' again the forbidding darkness of before shuttered his face, and again was gone so quickly as to leave a doubt of its passing '—well, I'd certainly provide for her to the—to the limit. I'd do all I could, and I'd do it without scenes or legal compulsion. Our arrangements would be . . . er . . . civilized. I'd want to remain her friend.'

She was silent only with the sense—now—of let-down and impasse.

'But love,' he continued against expectation, reflectively. 'I rather expect that love is like a plane crash or a driving accident—you can't imagine it till you're *in* it.'

'Very likely,' she murmured, bemused by enigma.

'Tell me.' Paul's voice was different again, mocking. 'Have I said anything that's worth a damn?'

'No,' she returned. As both of them burst out laughing, she thought how her disproportionate joy in this shared moment exposed indecently, if only to herself, her hunger for love, her daily poverty of love.

'All the same, darling,' she digressed resolutely. 'I don't see why you should be inconvenienced by this shotgun affair, for the sake of fifty or a hundred pounds. Do please let me—'

'No, no!' he countered as resolutely. 'Not for anything, Mummy. I'm quite all right—I'm doing jolly well, actually.'

He was doing well; she had never quite got over the anomaly of producing a child who was brilliant in—of all things— chemical dynamics, his future completely assured; he was one of the lucky beings with an unmistakable talent.

'Well . . .' she shrugged, defeated. 'Let me get you some sherry.'

'No, let me.' Both of them were on their feet; he astounded her by taking her suddenly around the waist and kissing her.

'I adore you,' she said, her voice carefully flat.

'You're rather a decent old stick yourself,' he said, and nuzzled her cheek with pretended violence.

'Tableau,' said a voice from the doorway.

'The cook—ingratiating myself with the cook,' Paul explained without haste. His letting go of her was also perfectly unhurried, but all the same she felt dropped like a hot potato. She sensed, likewise, Paul's annoyance before his father's faint smile and composed advance into the room, and marvelled— for one moment, and for the thousandth time—at Ian's ability to make a fool of her. And yet, a son kissing his mother, what was so extraordinary about it, so ludicrous? But Ian with his special gift of belittlement could make it ludicrous with hardly

39

a word, and by the same token not only could make Paul regret and dislike his rare moment of demonstration, but hold it against his mother for having evoked it from him.

'What will you have?' he was asking his father, his nonchalance restored a little too markedly. 'Whisky, gin—?'

'Whisky and water, please. Thank you.' Ian continued his amiable advance toward Heather, and bestowed on her the usual evening kiss. Her instinctive desire to jerk away from him, and her instinctive control of it, both surprised her by their violence. *You spoiled it*, she raged inwardly, *you spoil everything*, then in the same instant felt a calm flowing into her resentment, a strength virtually never there. And all this could harrow her in the fraction of a moment, she thought wonderingly, and no sign of it appear on the surface . . .

'Your mother's sherry,' Ian reminded Paul.

'In a moment, please,' said Heather. 'I'll organize dinner first.'

In the kitchen, two major considerations possessed her. First was the conversation she had had with Paul, and the sheer impossibility of such a conversation between mother and son as little as ten years ago; the second, more complex, was annoyingly paradoxical. She was angry with Paul for abandoning her both spiritually and physically on his father's entrance; she was angry with him for his instant surrender to his father's atmosphere. And yet the feeling their talk had given her—her brief moment as the friend and equal of her mysterious son—buoyed her up with illogical assurance and somehow purged her of her eroding self-distrust, her painful hesitations. . . . With incredulity, with actual scorn, she looked back at her cumulative dread of approaching Ian, her fear of petitioning humbly for some part of her life as her own. Why, after all? why? After dinner, immediately after coffee, she would open the discussion with her husband; she would be quiet but immovable, composed but insistent, she was through with cravenness. And Paul had done this for her; Paul, unknowing, had warmed her with this gift of confident serenity. Their talk, having nothing to do with her secret desire, had nevertheless lifted her to this plane of tranquil resolution. Strange, the unseen unpredictable links between persons and events the most diverse, the most dissevered. . . .

With everything done that should be done—the cooker adjusted, the electric cart turned on—she started to leave the kitchen, then checked abruptly and stood still, with recollection in her face. Paul: Paul's look when they had started talking of love, that single flash too quick in its passing to recognize . . . fear almost, but why fear? Or more accurately . . . consternation? the look of someone confronted without warning by an unfairly-oversized opponent . . . ? But her impression, more ephemeral than the moment which had produced it, faded to nothingness and left her standing there, wondering why she had paused.

When she entered the living-room with coffee, Ian asked negligently but unusually, 'I don't seem to've seen Chantal for a couple of days? Where's she now? out gadding as usual?'

'Out gadding permanently,' she returned in a brittle voice, and dumped her load with unintentional emphasis. Her mind, totally clamped upon the request she would lay before Ian, totally resented the inquiry as distraction, a threat to her carefully-hoarded resolve. The flag of her determination, however whipped by recurrent gusts of nervousness, reappeared always still flying; while relieved to see it, she knew it would not survive much more buffeting.

Now, remote in spirit, she was dispensing coffee from the beautiful but inconvenient silver pot over its alcohol lamp, set off by its matching tray, bowl and pitcher, massive and heavy; a thousand times she had cursed this bequest of Ian's family silver. Long ago she had tried to introduce the glass coffee-maker on its weightless electric trivet, an experiment that had survived precisely one dinner. Or rather, one single lifting of Ian's eyebrow, his single smiling inquiry, 'Like a caff, isn't it? or an American "drug-store"?' The very quotation-marks around *drug-store* had been audible, and from then on she used the dispenser for the kitchen, or occasional visitors. Ian loved particularly the panoply of the coffee ritual, the silver that must appear luminously brilliant, the spoons that must be polished with special care for their thinness and great age, the cups of old Crown Derby that required tender washing all by themselves in a towel-lined bowl, in aristocratic *apartheid*.

'Why permanently?' Ian asked.

Startled, she had to grope for the thread; mere seconds had detached her completely from him.

'Chantal?' She finished pouring a cup. 'Because she was lazy and irresponsible.' She handed the cup to Paul. 'And dirty.'

The three of them sipped the admirable brew, black and burning hot, in silence.

'You surprise me,' said Ian; again the pause, long enough to be disconnecting, jolted her from preoccupation to immediacy. '*Dirty*, did you say?'

'Well—disorderly.' Of all subjects she was disinclined to

canvass at the moment, Chantal probably headed the list. 'That's what I meant, of course—disorderly.'

'I thought you couldn't mean the other,' he observed.

'Well, naturally.' Beneath her rising asperity was a faint wonder at his tenacious comment on so alien a subject; unlikely that it could be construed into defence of Chantal, whom he had appeared to notice no more than any other domestic, but if not defence, what was it . . . ? 'D'you expect I'd have put up with *physical* uncleanliness? Of course I didn't mean dirty.'

Then why did you say it? Ian asked silently, and her ear, long attuned to his virtuosity of silences, heard him. Aloud he merely offered, 'So you've sent her packing. How'd you get hold of her in the first place?'

Oh Lord, who cares, she almost retorted with seething exasperation; these inconsequent digressions, nerve-racking. . . . 'I had a note of recommendation with her,' she answered composedly. 'It was just when I was crawling out of that Chinese flu, I was desperate for someone. Also,' she appended, 'much too seedy to judge—to size her up. I was only too grateful to find anyone.'

'Marvellous coffee.' Paul was holding out his cup. 'May I, please?'

She filled the cup, not only grateful for the interruption but belatedly conscious of his polite and patient boredom with his parents' exchanges over still another au pair.

'Thank you, Mummy. I should be pushing off,' he explained, 'but I'm not likely to be offered anything as good as this, all evening.'

'Next time you engage anyone of that sort,' Ian advised,

'better do it through an accredited agency—through people who regularly handle that sort of thing.'

'There won't be a next time,' she retorted, again vaguely surprised by his persistence; her own mind had conclusively shaken off the topic. 'I'd rather do a little washing-up than wear myself out hounding other Chantals.'

'*You've* been washing up—?'

'Only these last few days, the dinner things,' she returned, undecided as to whether her husband's surprise were genuine or spurious. His aloofness from domestic affairs was absolute, but aloofness in *that* degree—? Then, resignedly, she accepted it as genuine and simon-pure; Ian remarked no component of the household, animate or inanimate, except as its absence affected his comfort.

'But Mrs. Amin—?' he was saying.

'I'm not likely to risk losing a jewel like Mrs. Amin,' she returned decisively, 'by letting her find a sinkful of soiled dishes and pots and pans every morning.'

'Shan't I help you wash up, Mummy?' queried Paul artlessly. 'Now?'

'In black tie? Thanks all the same, darling—I only do the worst of it.' With a faint ironic smile she recognized this offer as a token offer that must not be accepted, and a responsive mischief in Paul's face signalled his complete understanding of her understanding.

'Excuse me then, would you?' he smiled, getting to his feet. 'Goodnight Mummy, goodnight Father,' and left gracefully, having got from her exactly what he wanted—absolution of his conscience by refusal of his offer, but refusal with perfect good-will.

'*Why* am I so nervous?' she berated herself some moments

later. Working at the sink in the stabilizing atmosphere of the kitchen, which stabilized her not at all, angrily she felt her hands turning cold in the hot water and her breath coming short. 'Heavens, he can't eat me. He can't *kill* me,' she argued with herself, aware of her real trouble—Ian's after-dinner discursiveness, his uncharacteristic talk about Chantal that had shredded her concentration upon a single objective; again and again she had had to renew her hold on a hard-won resolve, against the dismay of feeling it slip more and more from her grasp. . . .

'You can wait,' she told the sink aloud, and violently turned off the water. 'Tackle him now, get it over with. If I don't now I'll . . . I'll . . .' her unconscious muttering died away as she refused, by spoken words, to give body to the alternative. She rinsed and dried her hands hastily, flung the towel aside, and plunged from the kitchen.

Just as she stepped into the hall the sound, catching her around the knees like a lasso, halted her between one step and another, stock-still.

V

Oh my God, she prayed indistinctly, *Oh my God.* The phone shrilled and shrilled, and Ian appeared from the living-room. Obviously her look suggested to him no more than that she had just appeared for the same purpose as himself; she was glad he had not seen the galvanic violence of her halt.

He was repeating their number, his invariable fashion of answering, but broke off. 'A pay-phone,' he remarked, and waited; she could hear the pips distinctly, but not the succeeding voice. At once, however, and with slightly-lifted eyebrows, he offered her the handset. 'For you,' he said, 'Robina,' and turned away with perennial uninterest; he considered his wife's sister a scatty and irresponsible nuisance, and even her beauty had never screened her from his poor opinion.

Heather took the phone, for one instant delaying her answer as she watched her husband walk back into the living-room and close the door. That he of all people should eavesdrop was unimaginable, but all the same she was unboundedly grateful that all three extensions were upstairs. By the time she had said, 'Robbie?' the line was already strident with reiterations of 'Heather? Heather? Heath—'

'Yes, darling, yes, I'm here. What is it?'

'Oh Heather.' The voice was raw with panic. 'Oh Heather, he's *asked* me—!'

'Asked—?' Painfully her mind tried to wrest itself free of its one concern to grapple adequately with Robbie's.

'About that—you know—that Thursday afternoon. Days it's been now, more like two weeks, and that much later he goes and digs it up—!'

'Tell me,' Heather urged, with her voice alone trying to impose coherence on a woman palpably going to pieces. 'Tell me.'

'I am telling you! We were just—just sitting about after dinner—and all at once he came out with it. Didn't lead up, just—just dropped on me, just—*bashed* me with it.'

'What did you do?'

'Well, I—I—I tried to carry it off, said how did he expect me to remember, I'd have to look at my diary—'

'And—?'

'Well, my—my arms and legs'd gone all wonky, I could hardly move and yet I couldn't let him see it—'

'Yes?'

'—so I pranced away lightsomely and got the diary and said I'd been with you. And Heather, he—he gave me this . . .' she made a complicated sound of sharp indrawn breath, a gulp, a sob '. . . this *look*.'

A dead stop intervened; against it Heather essayed, 'Well, if that was all—'

'No, but listen, listen, I *know* that look of his, it always

47

means something and never anything good. And then he—he
—he—'

'Yes?'

'—he just took off—walked out of the house a few minutes
later without another word. And I was so terrified that he
might be on his way to you,' she keened, 'that I had to w-warn
you, I—I just tore out to the nearest phone—'

'But you don't know for sure that he was coming here?'
Heather interrupted. Unpleasant misgiving touched her, a
vague chill.

'He didn't say, he just—'

'But you've no idea at all where he went? No impression
even—?'

'I've told you, haven't I?' They were interrupting each
other on a note wound tighter and tighter. 'The first I knew of
it was the front door banging behind him. He always bangs
doors, it's one of his more endearing—'

'Robbie—,' Heather attempted.

'I didn't even dare ring you from the house,' Robina overbore her like a rushing torrent. 'For fear he'd had the phone
tapped or whatever they call it, it'd be just like him. I had to
warn you,' she repeated. 'I couldn't let him drop on you just
like that with—with some filthy trick up his sleeve, God
knows what. He may be there already, I've wasted too much
time talking about—but—but—take care, take care as much as
you . . . 'bye!'

In a gabbling hurry she had rung off; Heather stood a moment in silence, then slowly replaced the phone and slowly
re-entered the living-room.

'Another agitation of Robina's?' Ian queried amiably. He

48

had glanced from his book on her entrance. 'A worse one than usual?'

'Average,' she parried with false casualness. 'No more than average.' Of course he could have heard nothing through the closed door, a splendid heavy door of an earlier age. Or could he, on the other hand, have picked up anything here and there, a word too significant or indicative . . . ?

'She overdoes it, you know,' he returned, always agreeably. 'Dumping it all in your lap, running to you to straighten her out, all times and all seasons.'

'Oh well,' she evaded. The last thing she wanted was exploratory talk on the subject of Robina; if not for the possible menace of Hugh on the horizon she could initiate her question, avail herself of her remnant of courage. . . .

'Why did she ring you from a public phone?' he asked.

'I don't know.' The first lurching of her heart had calmed as she realized the query's lack of real interest, and the return of calm enabled her to discard invention. *Keep it simple*, Robbie's adjuration was in her ears, and she kept it simple. 'She didn't say.'

'Why not suggest to her one of these days,' he said off-handedly, 'that there's such a thing as a limit to imposition?'

Against the disparagement in his voice she sat silent, not denying her concern and having no wish to deny it. *If I had a daughter and saw her life going wrong*, she explained silently, *and couldn't help at all, I'd feel about her just the way I feel about Robbie. She needs me, she's unhappy and unfortunate and half-ill, and she depends on me. You and Paul don't need me*, she informed him, always without words. *If I died tomorrow it would make no difference to either of you, no real difference.* And still this working loom of thought was shot with

49

the recurrent thread of Hugh's possible advent on their doorstep. But for what reason, what possible reason. . . .

Oh God, she groaned inwardly again, feeling weariness to the marrow of her bones. The lingering sense of her sister's distraction and misery, her own consequent if vague apprehensions, were incalculably destructive—destructive to the conciseness of thought and speech necessary for her purpose, especially destructive to her built-up stockpile of courage . . . she must somehow reconstitute herself if the French project were to be laid before Ian . . . She started violently; the doorbell . . . ? no, her imagination. . . .

'What are you listening to?' her husband asked.

She started again, unaware that he had been observing her. 'Nothing,' she disclaimed. 'Nothing at all.'

During the next brief pause, over and above her need to recover from his question, a voice began dinning insistently, *Talk to him now, don't think, do it! If you think any more, you won't.*

'Ian,' she plunged. 'Ian.'

He raised his head from his book; his receptive politeness, customary, somehow relieved her tension not at all. Yet she must give no sign of anything but a confident assumption that she was about to make a reasonable request, to which he would accede reasonably.

'I'd like to discuss something with you,' she pursued, and followed his 'By all means,' with an unhurried, 'I'd like very much to study with a water-colourist in Paris.'

Now that it was out and the moment upon her, she was aware of a factitious calm that overspread her agitation like a skin of ice over roiled water; her worst fear had been that her constricted breathing would shake her voice, yet she heard it, as from a distance, perfectly steady.

'I see,' he answered amiably, and deliberated a moment. 'A bit recent, this whim?'

'No whim,' she returned. 'And not recent. I've thought of nothing else for a long time.' Some new unidentified thing touched her with steadiness. 'For the last few years.'

He nodded, noncommittal.

'And not dabble at it, I want to do it properly,' she pursued, having achieved momentum. 'For six months to begin, and later on, another six months.'

'I see.' Again he appeared to reflect, the fruit of his pondering being—after a moment—a very slight smile and the query, 'At your age?'

'I'm not senile,' she returned lightly, hardly believing her ears. Was *this* how he was going to oppose her—? 'I'm forty-six.'

'Hardly first bloom, though?'

'Even so.' In some sudden and mysterious way she was able to match his faint mockery with a mockery of her own. 'I've time ahead of me so far as I know, and I'd like to use it.'

'Undeniably you've got time,' he acquiesced. 'If your talent were as considerable as your time, I'd see the sense of it.'

'I shan't know if it's considerable or not till I have proper training.' *The meanness,* she thought indistinctly, her suspicions confirmed; *the meanness.* To fight her not openly but with these insidious weapons of denigration, belittlement of herself and her gift . . . the pinpoint of courage swelled suddenly to a bright anger, lifting her to a clarity of thought, wonderful: first, speculation on what form his further resistance might take, and second, her knowledge of being ready to resist him on all fronts, whatever they might be. Composedly, she waited for his next attack.

'So you've been plotting and planning,' he summed up amiably, 'in that funny little hole of yours upstairs?'

'Yes,' she agreed amiably, and waited again.

'A bit comfortless for Paul and me,' he suggested mildly. 'Knocking about in a deserted house.'

'Not comfortless at all,' she returned briskly. 'You won't be deprived of a single one of your comforts. Mrs. Amin is ready to take over, she'll do breakfast and dinner for you and keep the house as it's always kept. Nothing will be missing but— but me.' How perfect her excision of pathos from the words, she congratulated herself smugly. 'And what difference do I make? Paul's a grown man, he comes and goes as he likes, he'll do without his mummy for a bit, poor waif.'

'Paul,' Ian suggested to no one special, 'is a son.'

'Yes, but let's be honest. Where you're concerned, I'm something . . . just something familiar. Or even convenient,' she amended pleasantly. 'Convenient but not important.'

'Heather, my darling,' he deprecated with the smile that had always reduced her to pulp in his hands. 'Fancy your saying such a thing.' Now, by some secret alchemy of transformation, his smile was a brave front over unbearable hurt. 'Fancy.'

'Well, that—that seems to be my impression of it,' she returned lamely. 'For a good many years now.' More damaging than this lameness of reply was the appeasement in it, and she experienced the feeling of a traveller who has taken a wrong turning—a first check and disorientation, a first premonitory dismay of being lost. 'I don't think I've said anything out of the way.'

'Fiddlesticks,' he said with indulgence, rose, and walked unhurriedly towards her. 'My love, complete and utter fiddlesticks.' He took her by both hands and pulled, and she came up into his arms as pliant as an articulated puppet. 'Let's see how much you've grown,' he murmured in her ear. This had been a standing joke of their earliest life together; a slender nymph before marriage, she had grown considerably after it, grown up and grown out, to the great amusement of both; Ian would take hold of her and murmur, 'Two more inches around the waist since this morning. Disgusting—I'll rent you to a circus.' And now, as then, she was shaken by a gust of giggling, then laughter. 'That's better,' he approved, 'that's better,' and put his well-shaped mouth on hers. To the first kiss her response was withheld, to the second kiss not withheld, and beneath it all resistance and rebellion, beating in her unevenly like an occluded heart, fought against his nearness and against what it had done to her always and was doing to her now.

'Ian—no,' she tried to articulate into his kissing, the movement of speaking merely making the kiss more exciting and her devastation more complete; with only part success she freed her mouth and besought, 'No, please, please—let's talk.'

'Afterward,' he whispered on an attractively wicked inflection, tracing the lobe of her ear with his lips; she began to struggle and against her struggle his hold on her became stronger and stronger. Patently this locked striving was more and more pleasurable to both, and her losing battle was not against the mere common denominator of senses aroused, but against an enemy infinitely more subtle.

Her failure with her husband: her failure during her whole married life to find the key, the secret of release that would make him *belong* to her . . . with no exact idea of what this belonging was, she only knew it had never happened between them. In consequence, during all their married life, she had entered their every occasion of intimacy with a blind invocation of hope, *this time, this time,* only to hear it transmuted, with unfailing regularity, into *next time, next time.* Ian, for all his fastidiousness, was by no means devoid of sensuality; with this baser coin of love she had come to compound, while knowing by absolute instinct that sensuality was not the answer. For all these reasons, unconsciously she hailed each successive lovemaking as *another chance, another chance.* And now she was stripped to her fatal flaw, her fear of missing a chance; this was the collaborator and spy, the enemy in the camp. Simple, but by how many tortuous threads not simple, not simple at all. . . .

He kissed her again and she returned the kiss, the more ardently that this fervor of approach and response—in their punctual timetable of domestic sex—had not happened between them for years. Held fast, lulled and drowsy in its narcotic warmth, longing only to abandon herself and sink deeper into it she stood against the man, himself aroused, and thought, *What matters after all but this, what do I want but this, there's nothing else. What have I been making a song and dance about, what for* . . . Beyond the knowledge that they would be in bed in a few moments was a final knowledge of being fatally disarmed; her aspiration sinking into postponement, her courage seeping away past likelihood of another attempt, to a point of being lost forever. *Well, what of it,* she strove against an indistinct qualm that must be pain, *my nothing talent, let it go* . . . a dying flutter of protest barely reached her, a last despairing cry of something betrayed. . . .

'Anyway,' Ian was murmuring against her ear, 'I'd been planning a little surprise, a jaunt to Majorca or somewhere in the next couple of months, and that's the exact truth.'

A lie, flashed through her with electric, unwilled immediacy, *an exact lie he's thought up on the spur of the moment.* Her mind, shocked wide-awake, wrenched away from him violently; her body, more circumspect, merely went still —so utterly still that his surprise at feeling all ardour go out of her was great enough, momentarily, to loosen his hold and permit her to free herself, without any antagonizing abruptness of movement.

'Take your jaunt while I'm in Paris,' she suggested. 'Work me in if you've time.' As never before in her life she was furious and coldly outraged, understanding the trickery that had been practised upon her. In turn he had disparaged her talent, undermined her self-confidence, appealed to her sense of duty, cajoled her senses with lovemaking, and bribed her with the promise of a trip, all in the space of a few moments; and against this fluid and resourceful attack she, poor credulous simpleton, a loving creature unable to deny her nature, had nearly gone under once and for all. 'Visit me in Paris.'

'Well,' he said after a moment. As angry as herself, like herself he permitted virtually no sign of it to escape him. 'You seem to have made up your mind.'

'I have done,' she assured him.

'Yes.' His ironic look heralded a final hostile stratagem and she knew what it had to be; there was only one thing left.

'Living and studying in Paris for six months sounds moder-

55

ately expensive,' he pointed out. 'Have you thought how you're going to manage?'

'Indeed I have,' she returned crisply. 'I've a little money saved, not nearly enough, and certainly I don't want to make a big hole in the few thousands that Papa left me. I'm prepared to live very simply, and I take it for granted you'll make me an allowance. I also take for granted that you won't just *stop* me—just bludgeon me with financial duress, like a Victorian husband.'

'Hardly.' He was sharply offended at the implied slur on himself as a civilized being, an image that was his dearest possession; by giving this offense she knew, paradoxically, that she had strengthened her cause. Nothing could so effectively circumvent further opposition on his part, as suggesting that it was beneath him.

'No, using the financial whip would hardly occur to me,' he was saying glacially, as near to huffiness as she had ever seen him. 'A pity, rather, that it wouldn't occur to you too.'

Undressing, later on, a sudden exhaustion overcame her; she staggered and had to clutch at a chair for support. They had separate bedrooms, an arrangement decreed years ago not by herself but by Ian—not in token of a breach for there had been no breach, only in consequence of his undisguised preference for being a great deal alone; encroachment on his solitude when he wanted to be solitary was the one thing that made him overtly irritable. *The truth is he's a married bachelor*, she consoled herself wryly upon her banishment, lying heartsore and uncompanioned in lonely sleep that had made her sleep badly for a long time; now with all her heart she was glad that he was not there to witness her betraying enfeeblement, and still more glad that, in the estrangement of anger and defeat, he was hardly likely to pay her a visit tonight. 'It's taken it out of me,' she sighed vaguely, 'taken it out of me completely.' She was limp, wrung out, with a dull strengthless ache all through her. The knowledge that for the first time in her married life she had faced her husband down on a major issue was miles from elating her; in her victory she felt only an illogical sadness, fatigue being no climate for elation of any sort. *If I've got to fight for a thing, can it be I don't want it?* she wondered suddenly. *Or having to fight someone I love for it—then still more I don't want it—?* The conjecture brought in its train a dire corollary. *Am I going to give it up?* she thought, horrified. *After going through all that, am I going to give it up after all?*

She stood a moment, swaying, then beat off the hovering doubt. *Can't think,* she invented reprieve. *Tired as this, can't think at all,* and fell into bed. In the moment before pitching headlong into sleep, all at once she remembered something: her ear straining for the doorbell, portent of Hugh: his arrival, his undefined menace . . . in the stress of conflict with Ian, she had forgotten to listen. But the bell had not rung once, all evening. So after all Hugh had not intended to come; or if he had so intended, he had certainly not materialized.

VI

Mrs. Milland woke up all at once and completely and looked out at the splendid innocence of a most beautiful morning. Lying there unmoving, all but the life in her eyes with its changing nuance of depth and focus, there was about her—young no longer and with grey in her pretty brown hair—a reminiscence almost pathetic of girlhood, of morning hopefulness. She had woken happy, wondered why, and all at once remembered the reason for this lightness and expectation; her mind shied away from the leftover shadows she would not even name to herself, not on this morning of new beginnings . . . she closed her eyes again and lay half-smiling, till a rumour on the air of coffee-and-bacon fragrance brought to her face a look of increasing waking, then calculation. The peerless Mrs. Amin was giving Ian and Paul their breakfast; with belated and characteristic postponement of obvious recourse she looked at her watch, and was wonderfully pleased to see that by now both men, in the ordinary course, would have left the house some minutes ago. Just as well too; with

Ian at least she had little desire for an encounter, not at the moment. Had he come into her room to kiss her goodbye, and tiptoed out without disturbing her? She took leave to doubt it, she never slept that profoundly . . . his omission of the rite signified that she was in disfavour; well, she knew it already. She also knew that from now on till the moment of her departure for Paris he would surround her with this climate of disapproval and alienation, and that all she could do was weather it. An unconscious sigh escaped her, barely audible, yet in its minuscule compass were lament, endurance and resignation, all three.

Her face cleared totally; she was planning an orgy. The morning and the afternoon were hers, all hers, to do things she had never done before; to start the loom weaving a thrillingly unfamiliar fabric of *her* plans, *her* interests and intentions, hers alone . . . the instant she had framed this resolution, her face altered with irresolution. Ought she to ring her sister, include Robina in this unaccustomed joy? For as it happened, her sister was also her dearest friend . . . after a moment, unconsciously she shook her head. Robbie would be an uneasy companion, she would bring her troubles with her and harp on them, spoil everything . . . beside, the sight of someone else's unflawed happiness compared with her fretting and comfortless state might gall her with the additional cruelty of contrast . . .

No, she thought decisively; she would be selfish for once in her life, utterly selfish. And beside, she argued silently, one might share joy or sorrow, but not this one innermost thing; the fact of being born all over again one could not share. . . . In one sweep she flung aside the covers and whipped out of bed, her body still shapely beneath the delicate silk nightgown and her movements, if not those of the agile nymph she had been, quick and pleasing. She could come and go as she pleased without let or hindrance, she was free as air; on this her day, the first day of her new life, everything was working for her.

An orgy was what Mrs. Milland had intended, and she proceeded strictly along those lines. In a state of absurd enjoyment she roamed hither and yon, speaking to people at Air France, the French Consulate, the Lycée, everywhere she could think of. A first shyness hampered her in describing herself, a woman patently mature, as a potential student, but finding at once that the Gallic temperament was receptive and *sympathique* to precisely this sort of thing she became bolder about practising her French, and again found that she could navigate in rough and ready fashion, if not elegantly. At about two o'clock, footsore and happy, she discovered that she was starving, and by chance (again her lucky day) found herself near that infrequent survivor of the old English tea-shop, Bendick's; in this lovely haven she made an opulent lunch on their speciality of lobster salad, waistline-destroying tart and rich fragrant coffee, and was served by an elderly waitress (also a vanishing type) whose benevolent courtesy was in itself a pleasure. She sat stewing in well-being till a little past three, then crossed town again, having in mind some hard-wearing work-clothes unaffected by smudges, stains and dust, and with increasing langour—she was very tired—wandered vaguely through some departments at Harrods, but decided on nothing in the end.

It was close on five when she crossed the small flagstoned garden and staggered up the three dazzling-white stone steps

60

that were Mrs. Amin's hallmark, to her own front door. Her fatigue, considerable by now, could not impinge even slightly on her fluid boundaries of happiness, her new pleasure in everything. The evening was marvelous and very still, a hushed poem of Autumn; the sky brimful of a pale gold light somehow elegaic, the benign dusty warmth somehow evocative of the coming chill. In her handbag was stuffed a mass of brochures and leaflets, also she had bought papers and magazines and glanced through some of them at Bendick's; it was wonderful how daily advertisements of Paris accommodation, that daily her eye would flick over unseeingly, now took on the most delightful, practical and immediate application to herself. This evening she would write Dubost; if his answer were favourable she already had in hand all sorts of information on which she could move. The widow of a college professor sounded promising but there were others to whom she could write, beside recommended pensions; she canvassed these homely lodgings with the most absurd and thrilling excitement such as she never felt about the George V, where they always stopped in Paris. This *was* a wonderful day, the first day of her new life; in all her experience she remembered nothing comparable but the day of Ian's proposal and of her wedding in the beflowered country church, all those years and years ago . . . Putting her key in the lock she thought, *Je m'appelle Mimi,* and giggled aloud, a sound of young idiotic merriment.

She turned the key, let herself in, and entered the hall walking on air.

Instantly, on the sound of the door closing behind her, Ian appeared from the living-room. In this promptitude there was something so uncharacteristic that it pierced her dream sufficiently to initiate a process of waking while she stared at him, goggling vacantly. He had not hurried for he never hurried, he wore his usual expression that betrayed nothing, but in his general aspect there reached her remotely some element of . . . of urgency, disquiet . . . ?

'Hugh rang,' he said at once. 'He's coming over after dinner.'

Mrs. Milland fell headlong from her beatitude with a crash. Against her first sensation—of having the breath knocked out of her—she had an undeniable qualm of foreboding, and in the initial shock of disablement groped for, and rallied, her power of self-defense. Above and beyond all this was the knowledge that she must answer promptly and naturally, must not on any account let elapse the betraying pause of consternation, unreadiness . . .

'Did he?' she answered on just the proper indifferent note.

'He did.' Ian's hard direct voice and look made nonsense of her flimsy pretences. 'Also, in the hour or so that I've been home, Robina's tried to reach you four times, each time from a public phone.' His tone was of inclusive contempt. 'She was in a state, practically incoherent. Not that that's new—' familiar aversion thinned his lips '—but she seemed halfway to being demented.'

I'd better ring her, formed in her mind as the expected thing to say; his next words cut her off at the root.

'What's up, Heather?' he demanded. 'What's going on?'

'I don't know,' she disclaimed.

'You don't know—! If it's something as serious as it seems to be, you must know,' he accused. 'You must have some idea.'

'I haven't,' she repeated, and over the sinking in her stomach hazarded, 'It sounds like another of their rows—something worse than usual, apparently.'

'In that case, why come to us?' Ian exposed, at once, the falseness of her conjecture. 'What's Hugh want with us? With him especially we're not intimate, we're scarcely on terms.'

'I haven't a clue.' Her whole resolve, for Robina's sake, stuck like a faltering climber to a dizzy sheer; she must not look down, not let her clutch on the lie be weakened when in the end it might remain firm, she must hold on, hold on . . .

Her husband was silent a moment, his eyes and mind withdrawn from her and pursuing some quest of their own. At the end of this invisible journey they returned to her in no reassuring manner; she heard him before he opened his mouth.

'Heather,' he said. 'All this may be a storm Hugh's blowing up over nothing, but it's not his way. By his tone I could tell he was prepared to be unpleasant if not ugly—he must have *some*thing to go on, to be that high-handed—that offensive. Now if Robina's dragged you into something tell me about it, so I can at least be ready for him. Tell me, Heather, give me some idea what it is—tell me.'

'I would if I could,' she returned, over a stirring of panic before his urgency and his percipience, both. 'I've no idea what it's all about.'

'You assure me of that?' His voice had gone a little sharp. 'You promise me?'

'I promise you,' she said steadily, driven to the wall.

Between them fell a pause, very brief; during it his eyes never left her. Then with a shrug he seemed to abandon the

63

contest, except that she knew it—secretly—for the merest reprieve and no more.

'I'd better freshen up and see about dinner,' she said composedly. As she got upstairs by some unknown means of locomotion, for she could hardly feel her limbs nor feel them move, she knew that he stood watching her a long moment before going back into the living-room and closing the door.

In a curious alienation and remoteness, Mrs. Milland dressed for dinner. She moved with effort, spilling and dropping things and making poor work of zippers and hooks. Her nervousness, she told herself repeatedly, had nothing to do with the lies she had told her husband and proposed to keep telling her brother-in-law; it had nothing to do, even, with the prospect of Hugh's advent, only with her knowledge of the man's extraordinary vindictiveness. Otherwise her assurance was invincible that everything had been between herself and Robina alone; that there could exist no leak, no possible seepage through which Hugh could have found out anything, not about *that;* he must be coming this evening about something else, so all this worrying was needless. To this thought she clung like a limpet till the bottom fell out of it all at once, with a responsive draining and hollowness in herself. Merciful blankness took over, a fatalism stony and spent. *Wait till the moment,* a flat voice told her. *When the moment comes, you'll know.*

About to leave her room she glanced at the mirror and was horrified at the face that stared at her, its haggardness of pallor and tension. Hastily she sat down again and applied colour and more lipstick, a botched uneven job. All at once a voice spoke, unbidden: her own voice. 'Coward,' it gasped, with fathomless self-contempt. 'My God, what a *coward* you are.'

In the natural order of things, she must now enter the living-room for an apéritif. Accordingly she did so in all her usual elegance of manner, wearing a pretty dress; Ian rose, poured sherry, put it before her and went back to his chair, not looking at her once. The first sip told her the sherry was a great mistake; she got up, saying casually, 'I'll have mine in the kitchen while I'm doing this and that.'

He made no answer till she had picked up the glass and was halfway across the room.

'I forgot to tell you,' his voice followed her. 'Paul won't be in to dinner.' His tone was remote and measured; he remained concealed behind a newspaper.

'Thanks,' she returned. In the kitchen she poured Bristol Cream down the sink and re-entered the mindless void in which, however, she could accomplish familiar routines. Once, slightly but unnecessarily, she burnt her hand; the small vicious pain threatened her all at once with disintegration, a longing to let go and scream once, only once. She clutched the back of a chair till the moment passed, while thanking God for Paul's absence, at least; thank God for small mercies. . . .

Once again, after an ordinary and accustomed interval, she opened the living-room door and said in her usual voice, 'Ian? All ready.'

They exchanged remarks at intervals; what remarks she could not have said afterward if her life had depended on remembering. She realized his conversation as uncharacteristically sparse, and also realized in its sparseness his perplexity over

Hugh's impending visit. The few occasions when she met his glance were unpleasant; not that he watched her, he would disdain such an act as bad manners, but when they happened to look at each other his eyes were opaque, without communication.

On her side, the chief effort involved was the act of eating. Her throat had closed up, she fought recurrent waves of nausea, yet an untouched plate was the ultimate betrayal . . . in the end she must have forced down a sufficient amount, or at least when she rose to clear he offered no remark to the contrary.

The merciless ritual of dinner pursued its way; for once there was a blessed anaesthesia in the stately coffee-service and the trouble it involved. It was sitting between them in all its lustrous splendour when the doorbell went, simultaneously tearing the silence and rending her with a cold shaft that began in her heart and pierced humiliatingly through to her bowels.

VII

Ian went to open; she heard an unrevealing brevity of voices. Then almost at once Hugh preceded his host through the doorway, this promptness explained by the fact that he was still wearing a light overcoat and carrying his hat; all too evidently he had spurned the offices of their coat-room. She had got to her feet and advanced tentatively to meet him, doggedly and to the last moment observing the courtesies, like a marquise mounting the scaffold.

Hugh made short work of her gesture with a curt motion of his head in her general direction, less greeting than undisguised affront.

'Coffee?' Ian's offer, from behind him, likewise maintained the fiction of civilized commonplace.

'No coffee,' said Hugh. 'I've come for something rather different than coffee, and I'd like to get down to it.'

'By all means,' Ian murmured as she stood there at a loss, pointedly snubbed, an experience to which she was not accustomed. 'Won't you at least sit down?'

'Well,' said Hugh, and hesitated a moment. 'I expect I might as well.' His manner of planting himself on a chair with his coat flapping open about him made it plain that he accepted the offer in no other spirit than as a convenience to himself.

As he did them the favour of accepting a seat in their house, Heather regarded him like a doomed but fascinated bird; at every encounter with him, and never more than now, her mind strove with the endless incredulities and repulsions he inspired in her. By a fixed convention every human being is supposed to have at least one redeeming quality; she always ferreted in her mind for his, and after years of acquaintance was still unable to find it. He was very tall, easily six-foot-three, his frame broad and bony. His big head was bony, his big face displayed flat planes of bony forehead and cheek-bones between which thrust an arrogant nose, bony. His hair, a dark ginger fuzz, had always been unpleasingly sparse on his skull since she had known him, but seemed not to grow any sparser; his sallow complexion and pale wide lips were no sign of ill-health, for so far as she knew his health was indestructible. The fact that he ate like a pack of starving wolves seemed never to soften his angularities with any fat; often she had thought that his malice burned it off him, for his malice was of unpredictable dimension. As he sat there, a suit of admirable tailoring doing its best for his enveloping ungainliness, she also realized acutely that the most alarming thing about Hugh McVeigh—far more alarming than his unprepossessing look—was the fact that he represented in utmost degree, paradox; the paradox of reconciling in his nature all qualities reguarded, by tradition, as irreconcilable. Though a bully he was by no means a coward, though maniacally stubborn he

68

was by no means weak; sneering and spiteful, he was not so through frustration, for he was invincibly pleased with himself; offensively a braggart, his brags were never windy but solidly grounded. He had inherited a large fortune and again —paradoxical in being a rich man's son but no spendthrift incompetent—he had demonstrated that his gift for making poisonous atmospheres was only equalled by his gift for making money, and had so increased his father's wealth that Ian himself, a successful and astute businessman, had no exact idea of what it was, except that it was very considerable, even as wealth is reckoned these days. In two words a filthy rich man, a person irredeemably detestable, for such people exist. How could Robbie know what she was getting into, poor pretty Robbie with her headlong streaks of fecklessness, her aching dependence on love and indulgence, the sunny climates of gaiety and understanding. . . .

'I'll be brief as possible about this,' Hugh announced in the harsh dogmatic voice that went perfectly with his other characteristics. 'I've suspected my dear wife of various junketings for a long time now, but somehow I've done nothing about it—largely, I expect, because she's a scatty fool who didn't seem worth the trouble.'

Of his insulting reference to Robina, Heather was less aware than of an anomaly: that while these remarks were obviously aimed at herself, he seemed to ignore her altogether and address himself to Ian; this, for some reason, she found especially disturbing.

'But even a tiny brain like Robina's can overstep—carry things to the point where it's just that little bit too flagrant, just that little bit too contemptuous of one's dignity. So I did what I should have done long since—laid on a private agent to follow her.'

He paused a moment, marshalling his thoughts; still he spoke as exclusively to Ian as if she were not in the room.

'In the beginning I wasn't actually after chapter and verse, I merely instructed the chap to get me a general run-down on her stable of athletes, who they were, what they did—they weren't impressive, that much I'll tell you straightaway. Good-looking nobodies is the size of it—no money to pay damages and no reputations to lose, therefore small satisfaction out of suing them. So for the time being I held my hand. To tell you the truth, I didn't know what I was going to do.'

With an Olympian air he made this concession, that even Jove himself might nod occasionally.

'I couldn't seem to work myself to the point of divorce,' he continued. 'Not over my little nit of a promiscuous wife. Well, she's recently latched onto something a bit more substantial, a chap with a good job and good prospects and some small private means on the side. He'd something to lose, plenty in fact, so I thought I'd go for him, skewer him—have the fun of making him squeal.'

His enormous self-betrayal of appetite and malignant satisfaction, plus his total obliviousness of this self-betrayal, locked Heather in a more hypnotic stillness of wonderment. Was it possible that a man should so indecently parade his deformity of soul, was it possible . . . dazedly, even in the teeth of nothing good for herself on the way, she fumbled for the word to describe him and could find nothing adequate. . . .

'Well, I'd intelligence of her next rendezvous with him, never mind how—'

'He *was* having their phone tapped,' she thought. Robbie's

guess, that had seemed so wildly improbable, had been quite right.

'—he followed her there, eeled up after her and saw her go in, waited an appropriate length of time—' Hugh's narrative, flourishing along, came clearly to her again '—and finally rang the bell of the flat. In the pause that followed he heard vaguely a sort of scrambling, you can imagine—and once, unmistakably, a woman's voice. Then a man came to the door in a dressing-gown, and the agent asked to speak to my wife. The chap held him in parley—outraged flimflam etcetera—for precisely the length of time that would allow a woman to whip into her clothes and out the service stairs, then threw open the door and invited him in. No one there —of course.'

He paused again; a different pause, more calculated.

'Obviously I should've had a double surveillance front and back, I'd somehow overlooked that. First I regretted it. Now, I don't know.' With a sort of reptilian deliberateness he swivelled his head till, for the first time, he was looking at Heather. 'That was a Thursday afternoon, September 23rd. Would you care to tell me what you were doing that afternoon, Heather?'

'Why should she?' Ian put in coolly, the first word out of him.

'I haven't said that she ought, or that she must.' Hugh was blandness itself. 'I've merely asked her if she'd care to, haven't I done, Heather?'

'Certainly I'll tell you.' Out of a sort of swimming unreality, she heard her own indifferent voice. 'If you'll let me find my diary.'

'Do,' he urged cordially, smiling. 'Pray do.' *I've seen this manoeuvre before*, said his smile.

After a further suspension or waking sleep she was again in the living-room. How the two men had passed the interval, there was nothing to tell; both, sitting silent, punctiliously rose on her entrance, and again she had a vague sense of the headsman kneeling to his victim. Now she was leafing the pages of the diary, once asking in a natural way, 'The 23rd of last month did you say . . . Oh yes, here.' She read the scrawled *Robbie* she had promised her sister to set down, and had set down. 'Robbie was here,' she said neutrally. 'We were here together all afternoon.'

'All afternoon? and from what time, may I ask—?'

'Heavens, I forget. Quarter to three I expect, it's usually that.' Calmly she retailed what they had agreed on. 'From three or thereabout,' and all at once, even before his look of glistening pleasure apprized her, felt the deadfall giving ominously beneath her feet. Then, reviving, she thrust the feeling away and invoked her knowledge, her absolute and incontrovertible knowledge, that no living being could disprove what she and her sister had concocted between them. Robbie had not been seen in the man's flat nor she and Robbie overheard on the phone; Hugh was making his bluff out of something unseen and unheard. To that conviction she must cling however he tried to undermine her with his devious tactics, he was a master of deviousness. . . .

'From three,' Hugh echoed on a rising note, like a wheel humming up to high speed. 'Or thereabout, you say?'

'Yes.'

'Would you care,' he invited, 'to think that statement over?'

'Certainly not.'

'You say from three onward? you stick to that?'

'Of course.' She never glanced toward Ian for help, not once; by lying to him as well she had isolated herself from his help; out of this her own embroilment, she must fight her way alone.

'Be careful, Heather,' Hugh advised in a voice unnaturally soft.

'Don't threaten my wife,' Ian spoke up, calmly but decisively.

'Threaten your wife? even caution her? I shouldn't dream of it,' the other returned in dulcet travesty of shock. 'Actually, I'm trying to help her.—You wouldn't like to correct what you've just told me?' he returned his attention to Heather. 'Modify it? even retract it?'

'There's nothing to retract.' The exchange between the two men had given her a precious moment to reaffirm her creed, unshakable: *He knew nothing because there was nothing to know, he knew nothing, nothing. . . .*

'I'm asking you once more,' he was saying. 'Think it over, take your time. But be careful, Heather,' he urged again. 'Be very careful.'

'Thanks, but I needn't be careful,' she returned. 'I've nothing at all to tell you.'

A slight pause followed while Hugh, who had been sitting forward, let himself lean back in his chair. A horrid assurance suffused him, an easy ascendancy.

'Remarkable,' he said genially. 'Remarkable to find that among my dear wife's talents, is the gift for being in two places at once.' He turned on her a grin full of big yellow teeth, all his own; an irregularity in their formation threw his eye-teeth into special prominence. 'My agent never followed her up to that flat till after two-thirty, and yet she could be here before three?'

'I didn't say,' she returned boldly, 'on the dot, there might have been a half-hour's difference either way. One doesn't,' she reminded him contemptuously, 'time visits with a stopwatch.'

Another pause, slightly longer; during it her awareness was suddenly—and without looking at him—of Ian, and of his quality of attention. Though perfectly silent he was missing no word, no single inflection of tone or manner . . .

'You're lying,' said Hugh.

'Now *you* be careful,' said Ian promptly. 'With your language, and I mean damned careful.' Coming from him, a man who never swore, the impact of that *damned* was almost shocking.

'Well, well,' said Hugh, perfectly unimpressed. 'Call it however you like, it comes to the same thing. Your wife says that my wife was with her all afternoon on a given date, from threeish onward. I've a witness who can prove there's not one word of truth in it, and whom I can produce at any time you want. Now?' He looked from one to the other. 'This witness is outside, in my car—?'

'Yes,' said Ian at once; her own, 'Yes, you'd better,' came simultaneously.

In the silence that followed his going out, with no sound of the hall door (he must have left it a little open) her immediate feeling was wondering amusement. She knew the witness he would produce, for there could be only one. The knowledge inspired in her nothing but an unqualified amazement that he of all people—a man of ironbound common-sense—

could place his reliance on a witness so laughably incompetent, so certain to make him ridiculous in the long run . . .

'Heather.' Ian was giving her no time to pursue this fortifying vein of thought. 'If there's anything you haven't told me, tell me now.' He spoke quickly, listening for the door. 'This isn't the moment to hold anything back. Has that ape anything to go on, or hasn't he?'

'He hasn't,' she returned. 'He's been trying to frighten me into saying something, he'll stoop to anything, any—'

'I'm not interested in his ethos,' he interrupted. 'What I mean is, have you been telling the truth?'

'Yes,' she said curtly, then both fell silent against the sound of the opening and closing door and more than one pair of footfalls on the thick wall-to-wall carpeting.

Chantal's appearance in advance of Hugh gave her no feeling at all, except an incongruous awareness that her late au pair had dressed with great care for this occasion and looked unwontedly respectable. And—and something else, disquieting . . . poised? a little too sure of herself . . . ?

'You'd better sit down, Chantal,' Heather told her drily, and the girl, who had stood in a momentary ill-ease, lowered herself gingerly to the edge of a chair near the door, by choice segregating herself from the three chief participants.

'Now, Miss Fournier,' Hugh prompted from the armchair he had resumed. His look of assurance and authority was notable. 'I would like to ask you about a Thursday afternoon, September 23rd. Do you remember that day?'

'I remember,' said Chantal, and the two words alone were enough to affect Mrs. Milland like the clang of an alarm-bell. Chantal's English had had, always, a groping quality, a constant search if not struggle for the simplest words. In her present answer was no groping at all, no struggle; nothing but readiness, composure, and far less accent than usual.

'You remember,' Hugh returned. 'And why do you remember that particular day so clearly?'

'Because on ssiss day madame ssrow me out,' said Chantal. 'She told me she will give me till Saturday, then I must pack my ssings and get out.' While tripping as usual on certain tenses and sounds forever foreign to the French ear, she spoke with obvious facility. 'So I remember very well.'

'Yes,' Hugh encouraged. 'Go on.'

'And while she is telling me I cannot remain in her house, the telephone ring. And she goes in the hall to answer—'

'Yes?'

'And I—I listen quick at the kitchen door and I hear she talks to her sister Mrs. McVeigh, she does this very often and always they talk a long time—'

'Yes?' Hugh prodded, as she slowed again.

'—so I run upstairs *vite* to one of the extension, and I listen.—I do it,' she added defensively, not looking at anyone, 'because madame has told me to go and I am angry, *tellement pleine de malice*, and I think, I will do somessing she does not like—'

'No need to explain, Chantal, just carry on,' Ian put in, and his smile and tone somehow made the girl wince perceptibly. 'You're doing splendidly. So you listened on the extension—'

'Yes,' she agreed, and stopped. A new thing dragged at her voice, a shadow like dismay. 'I have listened. And—and—'

'One moment, before you go further,' Hugh interposed with his mentor's air. 'Mrs. McVeigh's usual way of talking

76

is very rapid, and when she's upset she talks even faster, and one might take for granted that—this time—she *was* upset. Now, are you sure you understand what was said? quite positive?'

'Oh yes, I am sure,' said Chantal. She had cast off the momentary impediment and looked cold and hard. 'I have been in school in England for two years, at Ladyvale Court near Angmering, and I understand English very well. I—I pretend wiss Mrs. Milland that I do not understand.' For an instant she looked shamed and furtive, but again quickly recovered. 'It is a way to protect yourself, so your madame does not give you too much to do. *Par example* she will tell her friends, "Do not try to give ssiss girl messages on the phone, she does not understand and she makes a *gachis*, a mess." So in ssiss way there is no need to write down a hundred ssings or remember—'

'Never mind that,' Hugh struck in irritably. 'Get on with it—what you heard on the telephone.'

'Well.' Chantal swallowed. 'Mrs. McVeigh is very *agitée*, *hysterique*, and of course I lose the talk a little while I am running upstairs. But she says, her husband makes a man to follow her, and the man has seen her go in somewhere. And he rings the door where she is with her *ami* in his flat, and the *ami* goes to the door and talks to the man, and meanwhile she puts on her clothes quick and runs out from the service door.'

'Go on.' Hugh's imperative voice had changed to a lazy relishing.

'So Mrs. McVeigh she ask Mrs. Milland, will she say she was here, in ssiss house, all afternoon.' Chantal stopped dead again.

'And what,' Hugh asked dreamily, 'did Mrs. Milland say?'

'She say Yes, darling, yes, I will say it. What did we do, *les courses*, shopping or what, and Mrs. McVeigh say No, ssiss is too much elaborate, we have remained *chez vous* and we have talked—I do not remember so *exactement* every word they say,' she digressed, 'but I—'

'We understand, Chantal,' Ian purred. 'You're doing admirably.' His smile this time chilled not only his wife but shook Chantal, again, to a visible degree.

'That's neither here nor there,' Hugh drove impatiently through the asides. 'The whole question—the only question—is this: did Mrs. McVeigh in fact visit Mrs. Milland?' His glance impaled his witness like a barrister's in court. 'Was Mrs. McVeigh in fact in this house, on the day we are speaking of?'

'No,' said Chantal. 'She was not here on that day, ever.'

'And how is it you're so perfectly sure of that?'

'Because—on ssiss day—I am just going out when madame stop me and tell me I must leave. So after she tell me I go out, yes, but there is no pleasure in it because of what has happened, I am too sad. So I come back to the house and no one see me, and I go up to my room.'

She paused an instant.

'Always when Mrs. McVeigh come,' she resumed with progressive fluency, 'she sit with madame in the little *atelier*, the little glass place upstairs, always I can hear their voices. But ssiss day nobody comes, nobody is talking, all is quiet. All that afternoon I am packing in my room or I sit there very unhappy—' a pathos quivered in her voice, speculatively '—and the doorbell does not ring even once.'

Hugh's additional admonishment, 'Now you're sure of

78

all this,' was purely a matter of form, and elicited the demurest, 'I listen on the telephone, hard.' The insolence that had flickered about her fugitively came out, for an instant, strong. 'It was very interesting. And I listen hard all afternoon, and nobody comes.'

A silence that followed seemed to carry with it some immobilizing power; for a long moment nobody moved and nobody spoke. At the end of it Hugh said flatly, 'Well, that's that. Thank you, Miss Fournier.' The acknowledgment was perfunctory, the dismissal absolute. 'That's all.'

The girl hesitated, palpably taken aback, then made a first movement to rise.

'One moment, Chantal,' said Ian, in a solicitous voice. 'You've been put to some trouble coming here, haven't you? My wife and I must pay you for your time.' His hand in his trousers pocket stirred up a jingle of small silver.

Chantal started to her feet as if stung; with face perceptibly paler and mouth fallen slightly open she stared at him. 'No,' she managed to get out. 'No.'

'Ah, I see.' Ian's warmth of understanding was even more deadly. 'You've been paid already.'

'No!' she repeated in a tight voice, husky and breathless; Hugh cut across her with another, 'That's all, Miss Fournier,' waspishly clearing the board of this piece that had served its turn, and threw in a brief nod unmistakably importing a later meeting. 'Good night.'

With sudden painful awkwardness, having no choice, she swallowed the affront in the face of the two men immovable in their chairs, of Ian's smiling regard and of Hugh's complete forgetfulness of her existence, now he had had his use out of her. Even a coarser type must be shamed before

79

them all by this brutal discarding; in Chantal's look, as she passed from the room, was so sweeping a fall from assurance to lonely humiliation and defencelessness, in her shoulders so sudden a cringing, that Heather could almost be sorry for her—if, she realized indistinctly, she could spare feeling of any sort from her own unpromising outlook.

VIII

'Mh'm,' said Hugh on a note of drowsy and pleasurable recapitulation. 'Mh'm.'

'Intelligent little girl,' Ian acquiesced, on a similar note. 'Looked up your whereabouts in Heather's address-book, of course, slept on it a bit, and ended by getting in touch with you.'

'Don't let's waste time,' Hugh addressed the air in front of him equably. After this he made no further sound nor move, employing the time-proven device—of forcing upon them, by his silence, the burden of the first worried questions, propitiations, the first explorative offers. . . .

'The next step is, obviously—' Ian's voice expressed no worry, and certainly no propitiation '—what do you propose doing about all this?'

'What do I propose doing?' Hugh echoed, with manifest appetite. 'Fairly obvious, I should have thought. I propose to sue my wife for divorce.' He stopped an instant, palpably for effect. 'And I propose to subpoena *your* wife as a principal witness to that effect. In this manner, you see, I give her a choice. She can confirm her sister's adultery, openly admitted to her on the telephone and overheard by my witness, or she can repeat the lies she's just been telling, under oath. And if she does that, she's perjured herself. *And* let herself in for the penalties of perjury which, may I remind you, aren't in the least nominal.'

Along with nightmare unbelief she felt a cowering all through her, where she sat perfectly disregarded by the other two; neither of them so much as glanced at her, as if the visibility for which she longed had already snuffed her out. Through this retracting blankness she heard as if from far away, Ian's voice: 'I see.'

'Naturally you see.' Hugh's concurrence was jovial. 'I expected you might do, after hearing that girl. To say nothing of the implication that your wife has consistently covered up for my wife's dirty little affairs.'

'And what,' queried Ian, 'does this covering-up and so forth amount to?'

'Amount to—! Have you ever heard of conspiracy, criminal conspiracy?'

'Criminal?' Ian's tone indicated little but theoretical interest. 'How criminal?'

'Have you ever heard of criminal intercourse?' Hugh demanded, ascending the higher registers of irony. 'Adultery?'

'Stuff and nonsense, my dear chap. You, if I may say so without offense, perfectly exemplify the average layman's wild and woolly ideas on English law. Legally, adultery's no crime.'

Hearing him remotely through a haze, even so she could

imagine how Ian's condescending voice must irritate his brother-in-law.

'It's not even a tort,' he was continuing. 'Adultery is merely a conjugal misdemeanour. Ask your solicitor, find me one legal work that defines it as a crime, go ahead. I'll pay you a hundred pounds out of hand, if you do.'

'You should have been a barrister.' In Hugh's retort was the hint of a snarl. '*You'd* be the forensic ornament, Christ—!'

'I'm no barrister, but my father wanted me to be one,' Ian disclaimed modestly. 'I gave the thing a couple of years' whirl, to please him.'

'That's neither here nor there.' Hugh's spurt of viciousness had passed. 'I've clear evidence of my wife's adultery, don't forget that. Don't forget my witness.'

'I don't forget your witnesses,' Ian corrected. 'Either of them. First let's take the agent that followed Robina up to this flat.—I take his word for it,' he fended off Hugh's attempt to speak '—that she was, actually, there. But have you asked this man, because any lawyer is going to ask him—' He paused a moment '—whether the chap in the flat answered the doorbell at once, or after an interval?'

'What—' Hugh was patently looking for a trap '—what in hell's that got to do with it?'

'A great deal—a very great deal. *Did* your agent in fact say—' Ian pressed his opponent '—how soon the man answered? Did he mention that?'

'Yes.' A grudging syllable, delayed.

'And—?'

'The bloke answered—' it was even more grudging '—at once.'

'Instantly?'

'Instantly, and likewise—' Hugh's irony revived '—in a dressing-gown.'

'And his look? disheveled, clutching an unfastened robe over an obvious nakedness? or—'

'See here,' Hugh interrupted. 'Of all the damned-fool, irrelevant—'

'Not irrelevant,' Ian corrected, 'and if your agent didn't mention it, he isn't worth his salt. What was the man's general appearance?'

'Well—' Hugh appeared to grind his teeth '—not as if he'd just popped out of the hay. Hair nice and smooth, dressing-gown buttoned up to the throat—a cool bastard, cool as they come.'

'Yes.' Ian nodded. 'A couple interrupted during actual intercourse—there's no mistaking the look of shock and panic. There's no time to comb the hair or fasten a lot of buttons neatly—these things take longer than you think when you're trying to do them in a hurry with your fingers shaking and your mind scrambling in circles—'

'See here.' Hugh was aggressive. 'What is all this damned nonsense, what's the good? Just what do you think you're telling me?'

'I'm telling you this.' Ian's voice was more than ever composed. 'That in the episode your agent interrupted, no intercourse took place. All indications point not to an act of adultery committed, but to an intention of adultery forestalled.' He smiled at Hugh in the most friendly fashion. 'Wanting or intending to go to bed with a man isn't at all the same thing as being caught in bed with him, or a lot of cinema-attending suburban wives would be facing divorce actions. No, no.' He was benevolent. 'Your agent rang too

84

soon—mucked the timing, I fear. He should have allowed for all possible preliminaries, let them get fairly down to it. Or his particular school of sex, perhaps, doesn't favour preliminaries?' His tone was sympathetic. 'In this case it's obvious that they didn't just simply fall into bed at once. Pity.' He shook his head deploringly. 'Pity.'

'Come off it, Ian,' Hugh exhorted harshly. 'You aren't putting me off with your quasi-legal flourishes. The fact remains that when your wife comes to testify in court she's between the fire and the frying-pan, and whether she damns her sister by telling the truth, or chooses to risk perjury by sticking to her lie, it's all grist to my mill. And don't forget my witness —don't forget the girl.'

'The girl, ah yes,' Ian agreed. 'By all means, let's discuss the girl.'

Could he be (she thought) as unperturbed as he sounded? For crouching there like a coward she hardly dared look at him, she only listened, and her dumbness she felt as part of her shame; she alone was the cause of this ugliness, yet here she sat with nothing so say for herself because there was nothing useful she could say, a liar caught naked in the fact of her lie. But to sit like this, humiliatingly wordless, to let the whole burden of her defense rest on another person, even if he were her husband. . . .

'Do,' she heard Hugh invite. 'Argue *her* away, if that's what you've got in mind. Go ahead, I'd like to see you try it.'

'I shouldn't dream of trying,' Ian responded. 'I merely beg to point out that if Robina contests your divorce action, her counsel will have had her thoroughly investigated before the case comes up, turned inside-out like old sacking. I don't expect she'll stand up very well to that sort of scrutiny, and still less to expert cross-examination. I should say that your witness, in the hands of competent counsel, will last about three minutes. He'll tear her to—'

'Rubbish!' Hugh exploded violently. 'Red herrings, Robina herself couldn't do better—!'

'By the way,' Ian queried. 'Where is Robina? Why didn't she come along?'

'Where's Robina?' the other echoed gloatingly. 'You suggest that Robina's got the guts to face up to the messes she creates? My dear chap, you do flatter her.' He laughed. 'When I told her what was in the wind she resorted to the classic refuge of the lily-livered—screaming hysterics. I had my choice of carrying her bodily out to the car, yelling her head off, or leaving her at home.' His bright glance suddenly included herself; without seeing it, she knew it. 'So I left her, wallowing in drama to her heart's content.'

Again, dully, a strange thought took shape in her: that in the sordid scene being played out, the stage should be empty of the principals, Robina and herself; one of them cravenly absent, the other shamefully voiceless; all the speech and action given over to secondary characters. . . .

'Let's not lose sight,' Hugh was inviting, 'of the main issue. Suppose they discredit my witness, how does that affect your wife's position in the matter?'

'It doesn't,' her husband acknowledged, and she thought that only a wife, even a failed wife, could detect in his tone a new capitulation, a first hint of tiredness.

'Robina hasn't a penny, so far as I know,' Ian was pursuing dispassionately. 'So in court, as you say, Heather can tell the truth and nail her sister into the coffin of divorce without maintenance, or she can persist in her lie, which lays her open to the charge—the very serious charge, to quote you again—of perjury. So in order to spare my wife this ordeal—' subtly his tone had changed again '—I'm prepared to discuss the matter on a different basis.'

'You interest me strangely,' returned Hugh, jovial. 'Pray proceed.'

'I've known all along it would come to this,' Ian said calmly. 'How much?'

'Well!' Hugh burlesqued amazement. 'Since you yourself suggest it . . .' He paused, ruminating.

'But don't be exorbitant,' Ian warned. 'If you try to bleed me, I'll be exploring a counter-suit for blackmail.'

'Watch yourself,' Hugh challenged, with a hard stare. 'Just watch yourself. I haven't asked you for a penny, and that I'll affirm on oath. Any suggestion of the sort has come entirely from you, not from me. Strange,' he sneered openly, 'for the legal mind to make such a bloomer—?'

'Come, come,' said Ian, also unmoved; as adversaries they were evenly matched. 'How much?'

'Well . . .' Hugh paused again. 'This time, say . . . two thousand quid.'

For mere shock she looked at Ian and saw his mouth go thin; the dark line of red that appeared on his cheekbones, she had never seen before. *No!* she shrieked silently. *Don't let him hold you up, don't pay him a penny. No, Ian, no—!* Simultaneously she was garrotted by the same knowledge, lethally disabling: that she and she alone was responsible for this extortion, and the fact arraigned her for a fool entitled only to hold her tongue and let someone else try to repair the damage she had done. This was the bitter crux: that by this single fact of responsibility, she had no right to speak. To the realization succeeded an equally comfortless comprehension. Hugh: Hugh and his methods. Just as he had postponed acting against his wife till she had found a lover worth ruining, just so he had swooped, an obscene vulture, on the opportunity of hurting as many people as possible beside his wife; his wife's sister, the sister's husband. . . .

'And cheap,' Hugh was pointing out gaily. 'Cheap at double the price, in view of barristers' advance retainers of five hundred guineas and so on.'

'I haven't that much in cash,' said Ian. 'You'll have to give me a day or two to sell something.'

'A day or two by all means, and I thought you'd laugh the other side of your face,' Hugh acceded jauntily. 'Charmed to oblige. It'll probably cost you a hundred or two extra in capital gains, to realize.'

'But before you get your cheque—' Ian was utterly impassive '—I require from you an undertaking that you will on no account call my wife as a witness in your divorce action, and also an acknowledgment that you've received two thousand pounds for so doing. One has to protect one's self,' he pointed out, 'in dealing with people like you.'

'You needn't worry,' Hugh shrugged, impervious to insult. 'Surely you can't think the lousy two thousand quid a consideration with *me*? But I thought it might be just enough to drive home a lesson—in the uses of truth, say.' He shrugged again. 'If you like, I'll write you your quittance here and now.'

'No,' said Ian calmly. 'You'll do nothing in this house but

get out of it. And from now on don't trouble to know me when we meet—I shan't know you.'

'My heart's bleeding,' said Hugh. 'You'll have your little acknowledgment straightaway—I'll even use a fivepenny stamp.' He heaved himself up. 'I don't blame you for feeling a bit sore,' he patronized Ian, after which the derisive grin he turned on his hostess comprised, by some alchemy, a withering contempt. 'Good night, Heather,' he said, and moved leisurely out of the room.

It's not the end of everything, was her first response to the sound of the street door closing. *It was bad, bad, but it's not the end of the world.* Arguing with herself in the asylumlike quiet that had succeeded the jangle of conflict, she was all at once aware that this quiet also had a forbidding quality. Yet against it—*Things aren't all that different,* she laboured at convincing herself. *Why should they be different, they aren't actually,* then looked at Ian; not as a matter of courage, only as something which could no longer be put off.

He sat perfectly silent, with eyes remote from the room. Even as she looked he shifted position a little—not in response to her glance, for he was not looking at her—sighed, and visibly returned. 'Well,' he murmured. 'Well, well.'

His sigh, unconscious acknowledgment of fatigue, was a sound almost unknown to her. Still with that sense upon her that it was not for her to say anything, that it became her better to hold her tongue till she was addressed, she found this humbling awareness joined to emotions bitterly incongruous. How superbly her husband had fought for her, how adroitly found means to defend her from the indefensible. And most humbling of all, worst of all, was the knowledge that she dared not even offer him her love, gratitude and admiration, tributes for which—considering their origin—he would have little use. . . .

Again he moved and sighed, and again she waited in her new subjugation till it pleased him to speak.

'Chantal,' he said in a musing voice, almost sportive. It had just struck her that something in this sportiveness was alarming, when his next words overlaid the half-impression. 'Takes it out of one a bit, these internecine broils,' he said casually, concealed a yawn, and glanced at his watch. 'Just on half-past eleven.' His voice and eyes discarded their last trappings of remoteness and focussed fully upon her, and she in turn compelled herself to meet them.

'About these plans of yours to study in Paris,' he said. 'I'd rather you didn't go on with them just now.' His tone was not peremptory, not even charged with implication—of which, nevertheless, she missed not one syllable. *You're not fit to be trusted on your own,* was part of it.

You're right, she concurred in her beaten soul. *I'm not fit to be at large.*

'Let's say,' he was pursuing, 'that it's not precisely the moment, and you'll give it a miss for now?'

'Yes,' she agreed. Vaguely yet unmistakably she understood that he was not claiming the blackmail as a reason for not supporting her in Paris. The loss of two thousand pounds to him, a man well-off, was not the point; the point was that she had to be punished for the mess she had made, and again, passively, she acquiesed in her punishment.

'Then for the time being—' by a useful convention he constrained her only with the polite interrogative, never the imperative '—we can regard the matter as dropped?'

'Yes,' she said, and waited for the pang. When nothing came she felt not even surprise; the toxins of shame and obligation, fatal to self-respect, seemed equally fatal to her power of regret.

'Well,' he said on a note of finality, and made to rise from his chair.

'Don't tell Paul,' she said without premeditation. The loudness and harshness of her voice surprised her as much as the words. 'Don't tell Paul, please—!'

'I've not the remotest intention of telling Paul,' he returned, and got up. The movement brought him into a stronger light, and belatedly she realized the colour of his skin, incandescently pale both with fatigue and with his fury at having to lie down under extortion. Yet as usual he was concealing it almost perfectly, and the knowledge added its weight to the weight of culpability crushing her down.

'You're ready to go up?' Ian asked courteously. 'I'll put out lights, shall I?'

IX

The interlude she had entered, for all its being a desert, was spiked with the thorny growths that pierce through in stricken places. The climate of this desert was loss, the loss of things she would only be able to name as she began feeling the lack of them, one by one. Yet this whole gamut of loss was enclosed in the single fact of the lie; her lie contained it all as an envelope contains a letter. This fact possessed her, at first, far more than the consequences that began succeeding each other, and led her into groping explorations of the lie as such. Her broodings on this, shapeless at first, began assuming such malignance of outline that they ended by frightening her as much as if she had seen a cancer endowed with a face and a body.

Not that the lie concerned her in its convention of immorality; this aspect was almost benign compared with its lethal core, which she felt as something sleeping, its nature and power not known till roused. Or again she felt it like the danger—apparently trivial, possibly fatal—of missing one step in a downward flight of steps. This was the lie's unique secret—its unpredictable emergence from hiding. Would it remain dormant by great good luck? would it manifest in a single revelation? in a series of revelations, with culminating power of ravagement? That her own lie—for example—had been from motives of love and protectiveness and completely without desire to hurt, had excused her no more than if she had told it with cruellest and evillest intent. . . .

In the end, curiously, her more elaborate imageries subsided to a single one, far more prosaic but equally comfortless. She saw lying as a gambling game, at which you won or lost. This game, like all such games, had stakes. Not the money-stake that one threw on the table, but the other kind—the stake driven into the ground, to which something is tied. To this stake the liar is fastened by the invisible tether of his lie, whose circumscribing length, forever unknown, jerks him back to his lie when he tries to pull free of it. And with what effect on his life or his reputation? Who knew? The inmost secret of the lie was its power of crippling. Take Robina, destroyed by many lies. Take herself, who through one lie had lost dignity, lost face with her husband together with an unknown proportion of his respect, lost her ability to oppose him and lost—worst of all—her single victorious stand against him as an individual having rights of her own. In the abasement where she sat, a clairvoyance of terror would sometimes take her. Suppose one day she were to see Paul trapped as she was trapped, caught and shackled in the lie and having to fight his way out of its discredit? With success or no success, who could tell . . . the chill that shook her at the thought was violent enough to shake this morbidness away. Of all people Paul, with his favouring life, his charm, his talent, was least liable to damaging circumstance, the lie included. Yet what if, what if . . . *I couldn't bear it,* she thought, then drove it from her. Why invent improbable miseries when what she had to put up with was quite enough. . . .

Also it was wretched, shaming and wretched, that in some perverse way the duel in their living-room should have sharpened her physical desire for her husband to a degree she had not known in years. That this desire was rooted in a slave's adoration she had no doubt, nor did she care in the least. That he should condescend to her out of the magnanimity of his strength; that he should raise and invest her with the dignity of his arms, his lips and his desire, sent a fierce thrill all through her, the crueler for remaining unassuaged. He was keeping his distance, always politely, and she reminded herself that few people value love, admiration or gratitude from a slave. Out of her new subservience she accepted as part of her punishment that annoyance and contempt had cooled him towards her, and only later realized a more essential truth: that she had been caught in a ridiculous position and had involved him in this ridicule, and that for such an offense —far more than for her deception—she could expect no forgiveness, not from such a man as Ian.

The final period to her pattern of subjugation she could never have imagined nor predicted. Entering her little glass workshop a few days later, for the first time after the debacle, again for the first time in her life she stood with dead eyes and blasted purpose, looking at the work that had been her refuge and feeling for it more contempt than she felt for herself. *This trash,* she thought, *this stupid, stupid stuff* . . . mechanically she sat down among portfolios and

94

folders crammed with water-colours, oppressive offspring of her low-grade fecundity, and wondered what to do with them. *Clear them out,* she thought, *sweep out the mess and have done with it. A bonfire.* She quailed, shrivelling inwardly like one of her own pictures in the flames, shrivelling and browning. *A feu de joie,* she persisted, while the irony of her lips was contested by the shape of a sob.

'Your technique,' said Mr. Burton, leafing through her portfolio, 'is unequal to your conceptions. Why don't you have a real go at this thing, instead of working entirely by yourself?'

'I've thought of it,' she murmured.

'A time comes when one's got to stop thinking,' he informed her austerely, 'and *do.*'

'Yes,' she assented, and continued to wait on his pleasure, grateful that he should look at her things at all; any gallery more impressive than this one would tell her of shows already booked a year in advance and no more artists admitted to their lists. Yet strangely, for all her listless awaiting of an unfavourable verdict, the sight of his mere discrimination and expertise of selection quickened her with a pale sort of pleasure. Ruthlessly and rapidly he was winnowing through her creations, sorting them into two piles, rejecting at first glance all the earlier ones, though none were dated. Obvious that he knew his business, and inevitable that she should hear what she was going to hear. . . .

'Well, I'll tell you,' he said at the end of his labours, and turned to face her. He was a short thick-set man with brownish skin, a long upper lip, and commonplace grey eyes behind gold-rimmed spectacles; his unpromising aspect was probably protective colouration. 'Some of these things are not bad, rather pleasant in fact. It would only remain for me to hang one or two—they wouldn't take much space—and see if there's any market for them. I might take that much of a chance, if you were willing.'

'Oh yes,' she breathed, too surprised to feel pleasure. 'Anything.'

'Well, possibly I might consider doing that,' he confirmed tentatively. 'Forty percent.'

'Sorry—?'

'Forty percent of whatever I can get for you,' he clarified. 'Any idea of what you want for them?'

'Oh no,' she demurred. 'I'd rather . . . I leave all that to you.'

'Well, that's sensible. You understand I can't ask much for them, since you've no name or reputation—? If you try to be pricey,' he explained, 'they'll be on your hands forever. If none of 'em sell at all you pay me a fee, depending on how long they've hung. Is that satisfactory?'

'Oh yes,' she agreed readily. 'That's entirely fair.'

'One other thing,' he forestalled her movement of departure. 'I can't display them like this, you understand, they must be framed. Not cheaply either, but attractively and nicely. A dozen at least—fewer than a dozen I couldn't be bothered with. Would you like to pay now for the framing? Might as well, there's no use wasting time.'

How like her, she thought as she left the gallery; how very like her to offer her pictures for sale, and instead of bringing money away, to have left money behind her, a fairly solid little cheque. Yet in the lees of her self-depreciation, however rooted, was an undeniable fact—that what she had offered had at least not been rejected out of hand. In this she took a pale comfort for the moment, till the other thought wiped it out and transfigured her face with melancholy. Robbie. . . .

Robbie, she went on thinking hauntedly; she had had no sight nor sound of Robbie since the episode with Hugh; every day she had awaited some sign of life, and every day there was nothing at all. How inadvisable it was to ring her sister at home she knew well, yet after this length of time she must risk it; by hook or by crook she must find out how it was with Robbie. . . .

The monosyllabic answer over the phone she took for one of the two servants that lived in, and asked for Mrs. McVeigh.

'Yes, Heather,' said the same voice, harsh and toneless; she would not have known it for Robina's voice. 'Look,' the strange voice was saying. 'I'll ring you from outside in a few moments.'

'Don't tell me,' the phone commanded, the instant she answered. 'I know. He came home and bragged about it. Roaring with laughter at the glorious humour of it all. And do you know, the horrible—the—the horrible part of it is—' she drew breath '—I mean, if I've got it right—he *did* make Ian buy you off from having to testify against me in a divorce court—is that how it was?'

'Yes.'

A pause intervened; after it Robina said, 'Now I understand how you can want to drive a knife into someone—to the hilt—and *twist*.' Half-strident, half-abrasive, she sounded more than ever unrecognizable; each word struck like flying grit off an emery-wheel. 'Because he isn't divorcing me, you know, or not till it damned well pleases him. Divorce me? when he can have the fun of roasting me over a slow fire? It's the best joke he's had in years. He just diddled Ian out of that two thousand quid, that's all, did it just for amusement and damn his filthy rotten soul to hell.'

Another silence fell; not grasping its quality, Heather strove, 'How are you?'

'Oh hell, I'm all right. What's it matter?'

'Well, darling, naturally I like to know and it does matter. Let's meet somewhere, h'm? wherever you like?'

'No.'

'Well, come and see me—'

'Set foot in your house?' Robina interrupted violently. 'God, no. If I ran into Ian, I'd sink through the floor.'

'But Ian's never at home between ten and—'

'No.'

A first unfamiliar misgiving touched Heather, a first symptom of being at a loss. Yet it was Robbie who was always at a loss and she who must always be resourceful for Robbie; this sudden reversal in their roles found her not only unprepared but considerably nonplussed. Often and often, hearing her sister's voice on the phone, sweet for all its alarmed plaintive note of a child running to be helped, she had thought with exasperation, 'Oh Robbie, grow *up!*' But the hurt child's voice was infinitely preferable to this dead voice, hard and cold and forbidding . . .

'Look, don't be an ass,' she cajoled. 'All this is rotten for me and worse for you, but if we can't see each other it's too utterly ridiculous—'

'Oh God, Heather, don't be *dense!*' Robina flung at her from between—apparently—clenched teeth. 'Must I spell it out for you? We aren't going to meet at your house or anywhere. We aren't going to see each other again, period.'

'What—what—' A wave of unbelieving loneliness such as she had never known toppled her for a moment; surfacing from its havoc she began to stammer, 'Oh, don't be a—a fool, you can't—you—you can't mean—'

'I do mean,' Robina struck her down implacably. 'We aren't seeing each other for the hell of a long time, and I mean it.'

'But Robbie—'

'No,' said the stranger with the voice of flint. 'I'm bad luck. I've hurt you enough, but from now on I can do you a favour and keep out of your life, and I'm *doing* it. So—'

'Oh Robbie, don't, don't talk like that.' The sound of her breaking voice horrified her; always it had been Robbie who lost her head and wept, and she who remained calm for Robbie's sake. 'Darling Robbie, please don't. This miserable thing that's happened, I—I don't blame you for it,' she strove, beginning to cry. 'I don't blame—'

'God damn these pips,' Robina cursed the mechanical cheeping. 'Wait—'

Heather waited in the paradox of sobs horridly wanting to convulse in laughter; the breaking heart had to postpone breakage till Robbie found a sixpence. The coin ingurgitated, once again she could plead, 'I'm not angry with you, you know I'm not angry, I love you—'

'And I love you,' Robina interrupted, granitic. 'Dearly. I expect you're the only person I ever have loved, except Mummy.'

'Well then—well then—'

'For Christ's sake don't harass me, this isn't much fun for me either. Now shut up will you, shut up a moment and listen.'

Against Robina's prohibition—helpless Robina's—it was strange that she dare not speak.

'Now look,' her sister commanded. 'I'm not running amok or anything like that, and you're not to worry. I've some damned good jewellry and I've got it where he can't find it, and I'm selling it and getting jolly good prices for it. And he couldn't get his big ugly hands on my car either, and I'm selling that. So don't imagine me plunging recklessly to the gutter, I've damned little use for gutters. What I shall do I don't know exactly, but when I do it, I'll have some money behind me.'

'But I've money, I can let you have—'

'Oh, be quiet,' Robina cut her short with savage fatigue. 'Knock holes in your pittance, on top of everything else I've done to you? It needs only that. So . . . ' A jauntiness, unbearable, came over the wire. 'The best of British, old thing.'

'Robbie,' Heather besought. 'Robbie.'

'See you one day,' said the voice, flinty and horribly bright. 'Maybe. 'Bye, Hezzer!'

But foolishly Mrs. Milland listened for moments to the dead phone, before ringing off.

Married couples were the staple society of other married couples, not by any immutable social law but only by natural gravitation. Of this social magnetic field Ian and Heather Milland were particles of long standing, except that in this instance the wife had not established intimacies with other wives, chiefly because her sister was her great and intimate friend. All the same Mrs. Milland, in her time, had been the recipient of sad and disturbing marital confidences which she had much rather not hear, the more so for being aware that she was seeing and hearing profound human misery which—for all her compassion—she was helpless to help.

Likewise on such occasions, beside her useless pity, two preoccupations held her. First was surprise that women she considered superficial acquaintances should select her for the exposure of these mortal wounds. Though beautiful she was very popular with women, probably because in her beauty there was nothing predatory; this complete absence of greed was an unrealized part of the tranquil façade she maintained at such cost to herself.

Second, after some such unveiling of a matrimonial rift was the curiosity in her, the speculation. In marriages so upheaved by disaster and yet—to her certain knowledge—not followed by divorce, what happened afterward? What did they *do?* The answer—after she had wondered and wondered, endlessly reviewing the myriad elements of any marriage—seemed to come down to this: they did what they could. They settled down to a workable arrangement. Of mutual politeness perhaps? polite mutual avoidance? Barren ground for a marriage, sad and sterile, yet maintained for a multitude of reasons—children, expense, the burden and complexity of uprooting a home long-established. . . .

And after all her ponderings on eroded marriages and what were the secret adjustments secretly made within them, it was ironic that she was being given a chance to find out at first hand. Not that her marriage had succumbed to the lesions of infidelity or cruelty, but the scale now hung out of balance; her status of equality with her husband had shifted, and not to her advantage. And what was she doing about it? What those other people must have done: adjusting. Not only the outer shell of her life stood impeccable, but also its inner workings; they were together as a family at the usual times and made the usual conversation. That Paul had no inkling at all of anything amiss was her solitary and reliable comfort. Still, of all people Paul was the last to remark the atmosphere between his father and mother unless it were very noticeable; beneath his attractive gloss of courtesy and easy friendship, Paul was engrossed in himself. To this old lonely knowledge was joined a new lonely knowledge of the sister she had lost and the husband with whom she now lived as an outsider. Mrs. Milland, like many people with an intense inner life, was not given to excessive talking, but she talked normally and adequately, with endearing glints of humour and observation. Now it must be her sense of exile, added to her sense of failure, that was shutting her into longer and longer silences.

'By the way,' said Ian, sitting with after-dinner coffee and brandy beside him and a book in his hand. 'I notice you're clearing out your little art-spot, or do I imagine it—?'

'No, you haven't imagined it,' she returned neutrally, looking up from her own book. 'I've got rid of everything more or less.' *Oh God I'm glad you don't know about the things I took to the dealer. When he throws them back at me you won't know, you or anyone else, I'm glad no one knows.* 'There's nothing left but my colours and so forth.'

'I thought there seemed to be less clutter,' he nodded, with tactful absence of approval. 'Well, I expect that one tires of most hobbies, sooner or later.'

'Yes,' she acquiesced, then surprised herself by saying, 'The place is no use but to gather dust, why don't you have it pulled down? You wanted to, when we took the house.'

'Yes, but—' he frowned slightly '—it was derelict then. Now it's been made perfectly good and strong I'd hardly care to destroy it—have the mess and disorder of closing the wall or putting in the right kind of Regency window. To say nothing,' he subjoined, 'of the expense.'

Two thousand pounds, she heard, as he had intended she should hear.

'Why don't you get some plants?' he asked. 'I believe there's a good bit of skill involved in taking care of indoor plants, it would be an interest. Also there's a lot of sun at that end,' he pointed out. 'With a mass of plants in bloom and sunlight striking through them, you'd have quite a blaze of colour.' He smiled encouragingly. 'You like colour.'

'Yes,' she said. 'It would be very pretty.'

He smiled again, returning to his book. Yet glancing at him she saw that this return was ostensible, not actual, the book had not re-engaged his attention; he sat mulling something over and preparing to say it . . . yet again, still looking at him, she had the curious feeling that she *saw* him change his mind; a process not usually accessible to eyesight, yet she thought she had seen it . . .

'Paul,' he said. 'What's up with Paul these days?'

'How do you mean?' she answered; it was a totally unexpected departure.

'I don't know, I seem to have the impression that something's . . . not worrying him actually, worrying's too strong a word—but something or other's on his mind—?'

'I hadn't noticed,' she returned, while it came to her that

she had been so totally absorbed in her own oppressions that Paul, even Paul, could be less distinct to her than usual . . . in compensation she offered, 'At his time of life so many things must be happening that . . . well, some of them might naturally give him a little concern, or something.'

'Yes,' he agreed absently. 'Well, it can't be anything serious. What matters at this stage is his work, and his work's going splendidly.'

As one might expect of a son of mine, she heard in silent corollary.

'And other problems he'd cope with rather well,' Ian was saying, with a shade of reminiscent amusement. 'He's fairly sensible.'

Not like some others, she heard again.

'I've been imagining things, I daresay,' he murmured, and during another pause sat reading.

'By the way.' His continuing voice, this time, brought her glance from her own book. Along with a sense of unprepared-ness it struck her in that moment—and never before, oddly —how often he used those words as an opening gambit. Also it struck her, again for the first time, how often they heralded something she had rather not hear.

'Have you,' he was asking, 'seen Robina lately?'

'No.' With the monosyllable she had a sudden and complete awareness: all the while he was talking about Paul, this was what he had really wanted to say.

'Well,' he pursued after allowing her time to enlarge on her answer, of which she had taken no advantage. 'That's something, at least. Have you heard from her?'

'Yes.' A dogged taciturnity had settled on her; let him pry from her what he could, question by question; she would

volunteer nothing. Her silence was less from conscious resolve than from the instinct of the wounded creature that
curls protectively about its wound.

'Often?' Ian had asked; she had to grope an instant before
replying, 'Only once.'

'Something else to the good,' he observed. 'Has that Pilt-
down man begun suit for divorce yet?'

'She didn't say.'

'Might I beg you,' he supplicated ironically, 'to be just a
trifle more discursive? Didn't she say what was going on?'

'No,' she returned, then elaborated with effort, 'She didn't
mention it. I think she was at the end of her rope, and *I*
wasn't going to press her for details.'

'She might well be at the end of her rope,' he approved.
'Well, she's learned at least one lesson—not to come running
and involving you in her idiotic messes—and high time. So
let's keep it that way.'

'Keep it what way?' she asked, genuinely uncomprehend-
ing.

'The way you're doing, the only sensible way after all—
the only wise thing. You'll continue to steer clear of her,
won't you?'

'No,' she said, looking at him with astonishment.

'Now my dear girl.' His pause, barely perceptible, was
sole admission that her answer was unexpected. 'Don't tell
me any argument's possible, after what's happened. You've
seen one consequence of being your sister's emotional
rubbish-tip, and need I say anything farther? Now please.'
Peremptoriness, faint, reinforced his tone. 'You've only to
continue giving her a miss, gently but firmly, and please go
on doing it. Promise me, Heather.'

'No,' she returned with the same level obduracy. 'I'll always go to her if she needs me. I don't care for what reason, I'd go to her always. She's my sister after all, my only sister.'

'Lord, Lord,' he sighed. 'I never get to the bottom of these imbecile formulas. Your only sister,' he echoed. 'What's the special merit of *only*? Does it confer some mysterious virtue on Robina? Does it keep her from being a scatty fool or a walking disaster? *Only!*'

She was silent.

'For that matter, I'm your *only* husband. Paul's your *only* son. So what? what of it?' Clearly her silence was exasperating him more than argument. 'Does a stock phrase like that entitle your sister to unlimited indulgence, however much she abuses it?'

Still deeply, invisibly incurved on herself in that posture —foetal—her silence was also not less than foetal.

'Please, Heather.' The command in his voice was now undisguised. 'How in God's name can you tell what that damned woman will land you in next? And if you can afford it at the present rate, I can't.'

The flying shaft struck where intended, yet seemed a little blunted—perhaps from the number of times he had aimed it . . . ?

'Promise me you'll keep her at arm's length, Heather. Give me your word, please.'

'No,' she returned dully. 'No.'

Awareness of this new antagonism, to deepen the standing trouble between Ian and herself, might reasonably be expected to keep her awake for some additional length of time. And in fact lying awake, according to expectation, she found her sense of the breach overlaid by a stubborn contentment. At least she had refused to make Robina a subject of discussion; to that extent she had protected her sister in her hour of shame and exposure, to that extent guarded her sister's remnant of privacy. Nor had she revealed her own forlorn banishment at Robina's hands; as destitute as Robina, she had not given her penniless state away; she felt the bankrupt's perverse satisfaction at staving off the inevitable revelation of bankruptcy.

When she slept, she had the most curious dream. She was standing in some sort of drab-walled enclosure without observable dimension of any kind; except for its atmosphere of barrenness and confinement it was unalarming. Out of this neutral vacuum spoke a voice, so perfectly independent and apart from any movement within her own mind, that this alone made it unique in her dream-experience: this quality of its being *outside*—outside of herself, outside of the dream. The voice as a voice was unrecognizable to her, with neither male nor female characteristics; all she could remember was the peculiar distinctness with which it said,

> *This is all*
> *Of lives squeezed small.*

It startled her awake, wide-awake as if spoken into her sleeping ear; for long moments its unbidden and exterior quality remained with her, nor could she believe that the words had emanated from herself. She must have read them, somewhere . . . ? except that for all her effort to pin them down, then or later, she could never remember where.

Unkind of Mr. Burton, especially after he had made her pay for the dozen fairly expensive frames. Unkind and unfair that he wanted her pictures taken off his hands after only a few weeks, he might at least have given her more of a chance, a little longer time. . . .

But the protest in her died of its own debility. Good news or bad, in such minor contexts, could make no real difference. Except for some calamity involving Ian or Paul, she was safe from further hurt; in this immunity she could take what comfort she chose. Even Robbie's empty place was no longer a desolation of pain, only an apathy of pain. She recognized that she was becoming resigned. She recognized also, from occasional uninterested glances at her mirror, that resignation was an ageing force, an accelerator of old age. Here she was, having lived her whole life so far in the family haven, only to find it no haven at all, no guarantee against loneliness, no bestower of warmth or safety in the hour of need . . . Well, well, it happened like that, to thousands beside herself; whatever her trouble, worse had happened to her betters. Curious that such thoughts should make lines about one's mouth, and curious that the idea should make her smile wryly and patiently.

Her first few steps into the gallery checked all at once; she stopped and thought involuntarily, 'Why, how charming!'

'They look rather nice, don't they?' came a complacent inquiry from behind her. 'Grouped like that, they're very attractive.'

'I didn't recognize them,' she admitted.

'I know—the frames make a powerful difference. And this is how I've done it, you see—displayed just one group of three at a time. And what I'm asking for them,' he explained, 'doesn't scare people off. So when a lady's interested I can always say, "Rather a pity to separate them, madam, isn't it, when they're so delightful together?" And I can point out truthfully it's less than she'd pay for one decent chair, and discuss them in the nature of an investment. People do love that word investment,' Mr. Burton confided. 'And beside, the consciousness of art nowadays is perfectly surprising. I said *consciousness* of art, mind you,' he twinkled, 'not knowledge of art. But the number of people with little money to spend, who like the *cachet* of a real hand-painted picture hanging on their walls, is rather remarkable. Of course it's merely a fashion. But a lucky fashion, eh?' he asked robustly. 'Lucky, that is, for the likes of you and me?'

She came away from the gallery with the first money she had ever earned burning, not a hole in her pocket, but as much warmth all through her as if it had been a fortune in-stead of thirty-odd pounds. Her dedication to unbroken bad luck had led her to put the gloomiest construction on Mr. Burton's non-committal ring, and even what he had deducted from her money, over and above his forty percent—'I'd bet-ter take off now for framing another half-dozen, hadn't I?' —was powerless to lessen the glow. And above and beyond the solace of mere acceptance, however small, rang the solace of Mr. Burton's words: *You've brought no more to show me? Why's that? . . . Oh now that's bad, you mustn't stop work-ing. Mind you I don't promise to sell any more, these few little sales may have been a fluke for all we know, but don't let your gift dry up for want of use. Not for my sake,* he had added *quickly,* peering at her. *For yours.*

And she believed him, and in some inexplicable way found this belief profoundly soothing, even healing. Grateful for his reproving little lecture, disproportionately cheered, she let a new lease of life take over to the point of reminding her: she had some small shopping to do.

The unusual crowding and strong current of movement dismayed her the instant she reached Household Wares; why, in this prosaic department, a sort of well-bred scrum . . . ? Then she realized that the press of bodies in the lift should have warned her, even before the signs: SCANDINAVIAN COLD TABLE AND KITCHENS, and for an instant she fought an impulse to dart into the next lift down. Then pushed by the eddy she had lost her chance, and before she realized had got into an aisle solid with people, where it was difficult to turn back; passively she surrendered herself to the thick stream that imposed its slow gait upon her and clotted—inevitably —first around the magnificent cold table resembling an arrangement of flowers rather than food, and then around a second table where samples were being dispensed. The exhibit was so arranged that spectators were forced relentlessly to circle its immense area in one direction, and being pinned fore and aft she might as well look as not. Studded along the exhibit space were warm living pictures each in its compartment—a Norwegian peasant kitchen, a superb modern Swedish ditto, tables set ready for the diners and exquisitely scintillant with silver, crystal and lit candelabra; the slow movement of the passing crowd made the candle-flames wave gently. It was a magic invocation of an ancient magic, almost an ancient religion—hospitality; created by a consummate selling-craft hardly inferior to stage-craft in forcing a response from the least responsive. Mrs. Milland, anything but unresponsive and still uplifted by her thirty pounds, began to admire. Easy to do where the least object was beautiful; she admired lordly casseroles, fluidly-designed silver, wine-glasses like bubbles caught from thin air; she admired the three blonde Viking goddesses almost too handsome to be real, who—in glorified peasant costume never seen on any peasant—were ardently pressing on anyone who stopped bits of smoked salmon or ham or sausage freshly sliced from parent sausages of Gargantuan size and august pedigree. She even accepted a miniature cornet of ham rolled around cheese and moved on, delicately sniffing its aroma of cured meat, golden cheese and subtle wood-smoke. The smell reminded her all at once that she was hungry, keenly and enjoyably hungry as she had not been for days; again she could thank Mr. Burton. Just having lifted the morsel, with her mouth actually in process of opening, she saw on the other side of the exhibit, and across its considerable width, Robina.

There could be no mistake; for all the contrived mellowness of the light, whose quality sometimes approached dimness, there was no doubt at all that she had seen Robina, and Robina had seen her. With no vestige of greeting or recognition, with a hard empty stare, Robina had looked straight at her sister across tableaux of gracious living, denying her existence and denying the moment itself. Mrs. Milland, with no consciousness of what she was doing, dropped the cornet and began to fight for passage the wrong way of the current. Blind and deaf to angry looks and acid comments in her wake she fought as a swimmer fights rough water towards an only objective . . . and when she got there of course no one, no Robbie . . . as she stood staring wildly this way and that in a patch where the crowd thinned momentarily, a helpful voice addressed her, 'Have you lost something, madam?'

'Yes,' she told the salesman too loudly, and quite unaware of the loudness. 'Yes.'

'Then if you . . . our lost and found department . . . on the . . . floor . . .'

'Yes.' His voice came in broken snatches, devoid of meaning. 'Yes.'

'A description . . .'

'Yes, thank you,' she returned in that loud mindless voice, and seeing a space opening toward the lifts followed it, thinking, *Lost, one creature, soft tawny hair and wide brown eyes, a defenseless infuriating child only able to feel the hurt, never to understand it or learn from it,* and found herself in the street with none of her errands accomplished. *Robbie,* she thought, trying to remember something; apart from the shock of her sister's refusing to know her, there had been something else . . . She had it: the change in Robbie herself, the frozen look of the once-eager and mobile features, the hardened, coarsened quality . . . and her present occupation of shuffling passive and lonely in a queue about a domestic exhibit however elaborate, for Robbie hated domesticity and in equal degree hated crowds. To this she was reduced, to herd with strangers and stare unseeingly at something in which she had no interest, in order to pass the slow empty hours, kill time . . .

Mrs. Milland was making for home like a wounded animal for its hole, as unconscious of her hunted gait as of the streets she traversed. With no thought of crying, it was consternating that at once, then every so often, she had to stop and dry her eyes. Yet as often as she blotted them the tears welled up incontinent, making her stop and take out her handkerchief, as determined to keep them from rolling down her face as if some point of honour were involved.

The last time was on her own doorstep; the wetness in her eyes surrounded the keyhole with a dance of rainbows. Ungently she dashed it away right and left, then could see to let herself into the hall—obscure even in daylight, as with all these tall narrow houses of 1830 or thereabout. In this gloom a formless alarm quickened her, an instinct outstripping actual sight or sound. Not Mrs. Amin, this late in the afternoon? yet movement somewhere in the empty house or on the shadowed staircase, higher up . . . ?

Another instant, and her blurred eyes cleared to the solid and undoubted spectacle of Chantal descending the stairs, with Paul behind her. Neither checking nor hastening at sight of her former employer she came composedly to floor-level, meeting Heather's blank stare full and flauntingly, with the faintest brazen smile on her lips. At the same un-hurried pace she proceeded to the street door and opened it; even while disappearing her back expressed the contemptuous amusement with which she shrugged off the whole thing and left Paul to face his mother.

The sound of the closing door, mockingly gentle, recalled her eyes from their last sight of Chantal and directed them towards her son. And what she expected to find was all there, the uneasy smile, the uneasy jauntiness, yet with it the over-all man-of-the-world air—the silent assumption that in every life such little contretemps were bound to happen, that be-tween two civilized people there was no need to raise dis-proportionate issues over them . . . Even in this moment, shaken as she was, it came to her how perfectly he was model-ling himself on his father's presumable behaviour in a like

113

situation, and how mathematically exact was this assessment of his father's attitude.

'Sorry about this, Mummy,' Paul offered. In the face of his palpable discomfort, his easy glibness was remarkable. 'To tell you the truth the girl's always pestered me, you've never noticed?—no?—and now she's by way of being a bloody nuisance. I had to see her here,' he amplified, 'because apparently she's got nowhere to see me. Only way I could rig it actually, I . . . ah . . .'

Perfectly devoid of any response as he began to run down, she nodded.

'So however it looked—' he shrugged and smiled, '—that's how it was.'

Without even a nod this time, she waited through mere suspension of thought.

'By the way, Mummy—' he hesitated imperceptibly, '—I'd be frightfully obliged if you didn't mention this to Father.' He waited an instant. '*D'accord?*'

She nodded, and saw obvious relief erase the man of the world and resurrect the schoolboy not so long ago vanished.

'Thanks,' he said, his nuance short of negligent, yet just implying it was no great matter after all. 'Thank you, darling.'

She nodded again.

'I don't suppose Father'd make a song-and-dance over it, it's not his style,' Paul remarked, with casualness completely re-achieved. 'Still, no use asking for it, is there?'

She detached her eyes from her son and her mind from its comprehension—a comprehension so total it was blank, with a sheet-lightning blankness. With all her might she held

114

at arm's length what she knew—what she knew, and wanted not to know. . . .

As she climbed the stairs, swaying slightly, the vision of her bed possessed her as the vision of the shrine the pilgrim. Once there she could let it all go—her little success that had raised her high, the meeting with Robina that had flung her pitilessly down, the encounter just now that had first startled, then somehow finished her. Once arrived at her bed she could throw herself into blackness, a marvelous unknowing. What happened after that would happen, and let it. Only not now, let it come later. After she had slept, slept . . .

X

Two lots of reprieve, afternoon sleep and overnight sleep, and every precious moment of them necessary before Mrs. Milland could gather herself to review, deliberately and without agitation, what she had seen in her front hall yesterday. Now, with wide unseeing eyes fixed on the first pallor of day creeping up her bedroom walls, she traversed the experience step by step—into complexities so numerous and so unforeseen that a first shrill warning seemed to go off in her head, an admonition to . . . to what? . . . to *recognize*, that was it; recognize in the incident's visible aspects, the invisible. And that these unseen elements were more important than the seen, was borne in on her more and more strongly; it was urgent, even gravely urgent, that she define and confront them. . . .

Unmoving, except for her shoulders' slight squaring against the pillow, she set herself to dismember the episode and miss nothing, however insignificant. Over the situation between Paul and Chantal there was hardly need to waste time, nor was she thinking of bed; something beside bed concerned her, if not clearly as yet. No need likewise to linger over her own blindness as to what was taking place daily and nightly under her nose; nor over the effrontery with which the girl had re-entered the house where she had done such harm, for copulation with the son of the house; all flagrant, yet having little or nothing to do with a more gnawing preoccupation. As mistress of the house outrage would have been excusable in her, it was even mandatory, yet then—as now—she felt outrage as a puny consideration beside the other oppression she was struggling to unearth . . .

She had it at last, the root of this heavier uneasiness; the shoddy arrangement between herself and Paul, to hide the event from his father. Her nervous start from head to foot that made the bedclothes rustle, signalled the new degree of awakening in her. With eyes still more remote, with a deepening criss-cross on the tranquil openness of her brow, she confronted her latest suicidal folly—of having conspired to keep a secret of such nature from Ian. Suppose him to find it out in some way or another . . . an additional heavy count against her, on top of what he already had. Once because of Robina and now because of Paul she had blundered into a quagmire, a fool incapable of learning by experience. Then quickly, without losing a moment, she must repair her mistake; tell Paul she could not lend herself to hugger-mugger of a sort which his father, if he discovered it, had every right to resent. Paul would be angry; let him be angry. She would tell Ian everything, make a clean breast of it . . .

Arriving at this only possible solution, she sighed with relief and let herself sink into its peace, into sleep or half-sleep —till some nagging edge, undefined, roused her more sharply than ever. What now, what else . . . with a harassed gesture she pushed her hair off her forehead and lay again staring at the wall. What could be worse than the worry of conspiring against her husband, yet even beyond this was something deeper, still buried and unexhumed. . . .

Again she strained in the hunt, driven by the curious certainty that it was not only desirable to unearth this hidden anxiety, but utterly, urgently essential. She knew or seemed to know only one thing, that it stemmed from the encounter in the hall—or rather from some part of it still unperceived, not yet taken into account . . . doggedly she set herself to shred it apart moment by moment, till the thing overlooked or forgotten was forced to reveal itself . . . her indrawn breath, sharp and sudden, signalled how sharply she had come up against the bedrock of her unease.

Chantal.

Chantal . . . ? Her first impulse to dismiss the answer out of hand, gave way as quickly to conviction. Chantal was undoubtedly her splinter, her source of continuing disquiet. Yet why, why? The girl was nothing, an unpleasant type bound to be in and out of trouble and equally bound at last to disappear into the limbo of her kind—the young who were poor, irresponsible, unimportant . . . jerked up as by a check-rein, she found herself compelled to retract. Poor, yes, irresponsible perhaps, but unimportant? . . . She shook her head unconsciously, belatedly divining in Chantal a something to which she could give no name. Force? some quality of force still to make itself known, still to be reckoned with . . . ?

On a sudden yawn and abrupt movement she turned in bed, turning away from the whole thing. This amount of thought over a wretched little ingrate, a biter of the hand that fed her, and probably promiscuous; instead of crediting the girl with overdone potential she would do better to prepare herself for unavoidable discomfort—of telling Paul she must violate their pact, then of telling Ian about their young Don Juan and his juvenile-delinquent mistress.

'Let me, Mummy.' Paul intercepted her at the kitchen door and relieved her of the coffee service. She followed on the heels of his graceful little action, trammeled with unspoken apology and with unfulfilled intention hanging over her. With no sight of him all day till this moment, she had had no opportunity to break the news of her defection, and in consequence lay under the stretch and strain of postponement, for it was unthinkable that she should speak to Ian without warning Paul first. If only that engaging young man had not chosen, on this evening of all evenings, to slip into the house very late and unseen and to stop forever in the bath while she reconnoitred nervously, and more than once, on the second-floor landing; then, when dinner compelled her presence in the kitchen, to time his descent with his father's and to stick closer to him than a brother in the living-room; as if—one might almost think—as if he were trying to avoid her deliberately. . . .

'I didn't want to spoil this superb coffee,' her son remarked, two cups later. 'But now—' he replaced the delicate objects on the tray '—I wonder if you'd object to my calling a sort of . . .' his glance went from one parent to the other '. . . a family council of war?'

'Call away,' Ian invited, amiable and amused. 'A tactical problem? What is it?'

'Well . . .' Paul half-hesitated, half-glanced her way; it

must be from her new demotion that she asked, 'Shall I go?'

'Lord *no*, Mummy! I count on—I mean, on you and Father both—'

His overdone vehemence, his charming embarrassment, his assumption of a manner far more ingenuous and inexperienced than his normal one; she acknowledged them with ironic appreciation as skilful groundwork, and wondered what other secrets he could have up his sleeve, apart from the one between them.

'The fact is,' he continued, 'that while Chantal was here she and I had a . . . a bit of a flutter on. I'm damned sorry about it, but that's how it is.'

Only with this disclosure on a frank, sincere and manly note, did she understand, or half-understand. Paul had correctly estimated her weakness as a repository of confidences, he had guessed her intention of disclosure, and showed her he had guessed by beating her to it. In his action was a thumbing of the nose, an unpleasant mischief and mockery that she felt with vague beginnings of pain. He might have done it differently; he might have said, *I'll tell Father myself, Mummy, I know it worries you to hide it.* Instead, he had chosen to do it this way, a way that—like his little courtesy over the tray—had covert derision in it, *poor old Mummy,* and punishment; he was punishing her. And yet in this behaviour was nothing she could resent openly nor come to grips with; she only perceived clearly that he was playing for safety.

'I don't excuse myself,' Paul was discoursing fluently, 'nor hide behind the fact that she fairly slung herself at me and that no one but a born St. Anthony . . . I mean . . .' he gestured. 'Well, the hell with that. It happened and I shouldn't have let it happen. I was a damned fool, no two ways about it, and now . . .' he started to savage his hair and restrained himself too late '—well, you can guess—and she's trying to put it on me—the responsibility—and I'm damned if I'll let her get away with it.'

'Mh'm,' said Ian. Except for a slight alertness in his eyebrows, he was non-committal. 'Mh'm.'

'Why, when she was still living here I'd cut off all that nonsense,' Paul declared, 'and I haven't even seen her for weeks—' he stopped suddenly '—except yesterday, just that once. She'd been hounding me by telephone, she wouldn't give up, and I had to put a stop to it. And a scene in a restaurant would be just up her street and I couldn't risk—and wherever it is she lives, God knows who'd be listening—so I made her come here, it was the only way I could think of to have it out with her.' He paused. 'Well, by stinking bad luck Mummy saw her leaving. There'd been nothing, nothing like that, but the look of it—to Mummy—I can imagine.' He flung back indignantly in his chair. 'So I'd be grateful for any hel— any advice,' he corrected himself, meticulously appealing to both '—if you'd care to give it to me. And if you don't, I'm the last to blame you.'

'Mh'm,' said Ian. Of reprobation or anything else his tone conveyed no least hint. 'Let me think.'

While her husband thought, Mrs. Milland sat in a suspension of which she did not know which ingredient was worst, the waiting or the helplessness. What the outcome of Ian's reflection would be she had no idea likewise except the certainty that it would be unacceptable to her, and that any attempt of hers to resist or change it would be useless. As to this family conference and of what had come to her unbelieving ears so far, she had only one outstanding perception—

of her son's cleverness. Clever of him to include her, since she had happened to see Chantal leaving the house—a fact which even Paul could scarcely play down; clever of him, while confessing the situation, simultaneously to evade it by beating a masterly retreat behind a smoke-screen of counterfeit inexperience; clever—especially clever—to present the affair on a tone so peculiarly acceptable to his father. Cunning, that was it, no more nor less than low cunning. Progressive disgust began filling her, along with something else so much in abeyance that she was unconscious of it; something growing, gathering, yet still submerged beneath her silent and intense watchfulness.

'Well, well. The first question that occurs to me is—' Ian surveyed his scion enigmatically '—just how much trouble is this girl prepared to make?'

'The limit, sir, I should say,' Paul returned with heartfelt conviction. 'The absolute bloody limit.'

'You're sure? with abortions being handed about like after-dinner mints—?'

'I suggested that.' Paul cleared his throat uneasily and glanced at his mother; his discovery that naked situations demand naked discussion was denting even his aplomb. 'I suggested abortion straightaway.'

'And—?'

'She wouldn't,' said Paul rancorously. 'She could've done, there was plenty of time then and there's still . . . but if she simply won't—' he threw out a hand and let it drop.

'Money,' Ian pursued. 'Have you—?'

'I did, and what I offered her—it wasn't mean I assure you, I'd no intention of doing it shabbily.'

'No,' Ian agreed. 'And—?'

122

'Nothing doing,' Paul returned, between savage and grim.

'Wedding bells or else,' Ian nodded, with dangerous amusement.

'And I—I apologize—for running to you with this squalid little mess, instead of handling it myself.' Paul was fervent. 'I could've done too, perfectly well, except—' he drew a harassed breath '—except that that girl, my God, she's perfectly capable of coming here again or—or even invading your office, raising a stink—I couldn't let it blow up in your face that way. Or in Mummy's,' he added hastily. 'So I *had* to forestall the possibility of some kind of—of scandal . . . Your name's well-known and important,' he blandished, 'if mine isn't.'

'Don't undervalue your own good name,' said Ian drily. 'It's all a man's got, when it comes down to it.'

'Well yes. But—'

'One moment,' Ian checked him. 'Just a moment.'

Again a pause contained Ian's cogitation, and again it contained his wife's emotion that was fast mounting to rage—volcanic pressure of rage that by some miracle had blown, as yet, no rifts of escape in her uncommenting calm and silence. Yet it was not control that held these intact, only sheer astonishment—sheer gaping paralysis of unbelief.

'Well.' Ian had emerged from reflection. 'As a problem, it doesn't sound insuperable.'

She had no need to look at Paul; without a glance she felt his instant hope, his lessening of tension.

'The girl,' Ian was saying. 'Where does she live?'

Paul hesitated.

'Here and there, I expect?' Ian answered for him. 'Dodges about from one hole to another—?'

Paul was silent.

'God knows where or with whom?' Ian continued the process of asking and answering his own questions. 'So that it's never easy to find her?'

'Well—' Paul hesitated again '—I can always find her.'

'She'd see to that,' Ian concurred. 'By telephone of course?'

Paul nodded.

'Of course,' his father repeated, smiling. 'Have you got this fly-by-night's current number?'

'Oh yes.'

'Well.' The senior Milland thought another moment. 'I can think of a number of approaches, all of them useful. All of them, in fact, damned good. Telephone Enquiries'll give you the little slut's address, and I'll have a private agent run down her way of life in general and her legal status in particular. Either we get her slung out of the country for vagrancy or delinquency, or we find she's here illegally, with the same result—' he checked thoughtfully. 'However, it's not a bad idea to have professional advice. Better come to my office at eleven tomorrow morning, would you, and we'll have a solicitor's view of it—I'll tell him it's by way of being an emergency.'

'Thank you, sir.'

Through Paul's gratitude she could hear something infinitely removed from gratitude—the stark and plain avowal that he was not hers but Ian's, all Ian's; they thought and felt alike.

'You might—I mean both of you—have torn strips off me and I'd have deserved every bit of it,' the penitent was continuing. 'I'm—I'm grateful, and I apologize again for—'

'Don't apologize,' Ian cut him off. 'You've done the only sensible thing, you've taken hold of it in time. Any other way it might have run out of control altogether—à la News of the World, anything. The one favour I do ask you—' he paused

'—these little gallops are dicey at best and expensive at worst. So don't make a habit of them, I beg.'

'No fear,' Paul returned cockily. Between him and his father glinted the ancient male freemasonry, the acknowledgment of the threadbare joke or at worst inconvenience, to be handled out of the way as expeditiously as possible. It was this expression on both faces—those faint man-to-man grins—that roused Mrs. Milland from her listening trance to a rage of which she would not have believed herself capable.

'Well.' Paul, buoyant and free as air, stood up. 'Well, I'll be off. Eleven tomorrow morning? And thank you again. Goodnight, sir, goodnight, Mummy.' He disappeared, too blithe with virtual guarantee of escape to notice the rigidity, the faint recoil almost, with which his mother sustained his kiss.

'Young scamp,' Ian murmured to himself, still smiling. 'Mh'm.' He abandoned his soliloquy of lingering amusement to accuse her directly, 'And it was going on under your nose, all the time.'

'It doesn't matter,' she flung at him; it had taken only his tinge of reproach to detonate all her stored lightning. 'It's not what happened then—or how—or when. None of that matters.' Her breath was coming short, not from nervousness or her old hampering timidity, but from anger; in her anger she was fearless. 'It's only now that matters—*now*.'

'As you say.' He was interpreting her indignation for championship of Paul. 'Talk about nursing a viper—! Well, our Chantal's got a lesson to learn.' A purring was in his voice, an anticipation. 'Not a nice lesson.'

'What's that to do with it?' she exploded all at once.

'What's that to do with—with anything, with—' Too beset with crowding details to pick and choose, she seized on the nearest at hand. 'To begin with he was lying.' She made no attempt to soften it. 'Paul was lying.'

'Lying?' Ian repeated after a moment without belief, unbelief nor even challenge; he had to recover from a first surprise at his wife's unwonted violence. 'Lying about what?'

'About when I caught her leaving the house,' she returned. 'He had to admit it by way of keeping me quiet—it was a fairly good effort. Not good enough though, for anyone who'd seen them. "He'd got her here to have it out with her!"' scornfully she quoted her son. 'He lied to me then, and he's lied to you now.'

'What do you mean?' Ian returned, with a first demand.

'I mean they'd been to bed together. Don't tell me that I or anyone with a grain of sense could mistake that atmosphere.' She drew a harsh breath. 'Then after bed they'd had a row, a bad one, and you couldn't mistake that either.' She gulped for air, seeing again the picture in the unlit hall—the girl hostile in her lowering beauty, the man hostile through his aura of recent physical satiation, the hatred in the air almost visible, thickened and darkened with recent sex. 'When he said he'd had nothing to do with her for months he was lying, don't you *see?*'

'Well, but . . .' Ian was obviously perplexed; not often that she succeeded in perplexing him. '. . . even so it's a detail, a mere detail—'

'Detail!' she interrupted. 'Very good, if he's lying about a detail, why shouldn't he be lying about all of it? I don't believe a word he's said, not a single word—!'

'A young man.' Ian shrugged. 'He'll try to minimize his indiscretions every time, or get out of them. It's human nature.'

'It's male human nature,' she retorted, and passingly regretted the schoolgirl riposte. 'In any case, in all this there's one point that matters, one single point, and I've yet to hear it mentioned—not by you, not by Paul. Not once! not even once!—'

'What are you—' his bewilderment was not simulated '—what *are* you talking about?'

'I'm talking about the single important issue in this affair—the one important question. I listened and listened for it, every moment I thought you were going to ask it. And you didn't!' she accused. 'You never asked—!'

'Ask?' he cut across her. 'Ask what?'

'If the child were in fact his!' she shot at him. 'If the child were Paul's. Why didn't you ask him? Why not?'

'Well, you needn't shout.' In his soothing voice was still unfeigned wonderment. 'Why should I have asked? What difference does it make?'

'What—what difference!' she gasped, her voice failing for an instant. 'But supposing the child is Paul's, what then? what then?'

'Why, nothing.' His composure was again intact. 'If this by-blow is Paul's, all the more reason to extricate him from the entanglement. Surely you don't fancy Paul's progeny by Chantal?' Something happened in his face. 'By that little whore? I know I don't.'

She's never struck me as a whore, she almost said; mere surprise at her intention kept her quiet.

'So that's why I didn't ask this desperately important question of yours,' Ian continued calmly. 'Because I don't give a tinker's curse whether it's Paul's child or not. If it is, the rotten heredity on one side makes it all the more urgent to get him out of the mess. I'm not seeing him with a millstone around his neck, all for a spot of youthful fun.'

'What about her?' she challenged. 'What about the girl?'

'What about . . .' His voice died incredulously; he stared at her. 'Heather, what ails you? Has the girl deserved so well of you that you're taking up the cudgels in her behalf? Don't be a fool, I beg you—not again.'

'I . . .' That *again* had checked her badly. 'No, she's de-served nothing, most likely.' She shook off the cruel reminder. 'Perhaps I should hate her, I don't know, it doesn't seem im-portant whether I do or not. The—the important thing—'

'All this,' he put in as she fought for words, 'over a promis-cuous little—'

'She's a young girl!' she gainsaid loudly. 'She's a living be-ing, not a sack of potatoes! She's in a frightful situation, she's poor, she's probably friendless, and you're preparing to hound her and disgrace her—'

'Any disgrace,' he corrected her, 'has been well and truly earned long ago, by Chantal herself. Since that bright caper of hers with Hugh I've had her rather constantly in mind, but didn't know quite what to do. Well, now I do know. I know, all right.' Again the constriction was in his face, a look of flesh actually shrinking on bone, and there struck her an impression, a future incongruity: that so handsome a man might, by force of time, shrivel to a mean-looking old man. 'And believe me, I'm not losing the chance.'

'I—I don't believe she's promiscuous.' With weak and scat-tered weapons she fought on disjointedly. 'She—she—' All at once that past perception of hers, unfocussed, revived strong and distinct. 'I think she's a considerable person in her own

128

right. I think she comes of good stock, there's something about her that—'

'For God's sake,' he interrupted with a degree of exasperation rare with him. 'She's a treacherous little rat who's—'

'That's not the point!' she shouted.

'I've asked you not to shout!' he shouted back; such accents had never ricocheted off the walls of their gently-bred living-room. 'She's asked for what she's going to get and she'll get it—'

'That's not what I'm talking about,' she broke in violently, and with equal violence he demanded, 'What in God's name *are* you talking about?'

'The child!' she clamoured. 'The child's all that matters, trust a man to miss the single important point. It's Paul's child, I'll swear it because he's done nothing so far but lie—lie to you in my presence, in the face of what he knew I'd seen with my own eyes. And relying either on Mummy's being too simple to know what she'd seen, or on her keeping quiet about it, the insolence! Also I'll swear the child's Paul's because *she* strikes me as—as more reliable than Paul. She's acted badly, yes, but that's not all there is to her, there're other—'

'God.' His invocation was a profundity of disgust. 'God.'

'God won't alter the fact that the child's a person, someone on the way. How do you lawyers say it?' she mocked perilously. '*In esse?* The child exists, it *is*, it's a fact you can't deny—!'

'Who's denying the little bastard?' he countered. 'And would you for God's sake tell me what you're getting at? What do you want?'

'I—I want—' the demand, its flat-of-the-hand impact, stopped her dead; she took a moment to recover and said, 'I think the only thing is—for Paul to marry her.'

Silence, thunderstruck and absolute, filled her ears and her consciousness; after it—

'Are you mad?' Ian asked softly. 'Have you taken complete leave of your senses?'

'And if he doesn't?' she struggled on with lessened fluency. 'Do you like the thought of the child trailing about with his mother to this and that assistance bureau? Do you like that picture? Because I don't—!'

'The girl's a strapping wench,' he shrugged. 'She'll work.'

'And leave the child at a *maternelle* or a cheap nursery where they stuff them with starches all day to keep them heavy and quiet? If they marry at least the child's somebody, he's got status. Let them divorce afterward by all means, but at least the child has identity, he has rights, he—'

'Heather.' His voice bore hers down with a weight of deadly gentleness. 'Haven't you made enough trouble already?'

Annihilated, she went dumb.

'I've put up with your sloppy arguments,' he continued with the same gentleness, 'but now I've had as much as I can take.'

Indeed, her mind acquiesced dully, it was remarkable that he had heard her out this far.

'I'm handling this,' he pursued inexorably, 'and you're going to keep out of it, entirely out of it, you understand?'

She was bankrupt of answer.

'And if I catch you trying to influence Paul, or meddling otherwise—' he drew breath harshly '—I think I'd leave you.'

'Do,' she invited with sudden stridency, then at once was light-headed with terror. 'Do.'

They stared at each other a moment, equally mired in impasse. For all the discord between them he was far from want-

130

ing his home broken up; for all her violence of retort, she was even farther from wanting it.

'So remember,' he said, after another pause; with one accord they were retreating from his insincere threat and her insincere counter-threat. 'I'm taking care of this, I'll deal with Chantal.' Across his face she seemed to see a running fissure, a venom of concentrated reprisal. 'You've nothing whatever to do with it, and I warn you not to interfere. Remember, Heather.' He paused another instant. 'Remember.'

It must be the quietness of his voice, she thought numbly, that had stripped her bare of everything; of anger, of resistance, of ability to fight back. She was empty and useless, hollow with defeat. . . .

'You're going up?' he queried, at her vague movement towards the door.

'Yes I—I think I shall.'

'I'll read a bit longer,' he said. 'Goodnight.'

She never understood then or afterward what moved her; the waking somnambulism or other exterior compulsion that carried her past the first floor and sent her upstairs to the second, long in advance of definite purpose within herself. On this floor, exclusively Paul's, were his bedroom, bath and sitting-room. Strange how unfamiliar this domain appeared to her, but Mrs. Amin's impeccable maintenance made supervision or inspection gratuitous to the point where any entrance of hers was trespass of one kind or another—unwanted maternal solicitude or mere thrusting curiosity. Actually, by habit of this knowledge, she dreamed almost as little of setting foot here as in the private flat of a tenant. But the resistless urgency of now, this *now*. . . .

In the hall, dimly lighted, the same mindless compulsion was pushing her towards the half-open door of his bedroom. Here he had left another small light burning; she closed the door noiselessly and stood a moment, trying to master her sense of gross intrusion and degrading furtiveness. Only after looking at the curtains and seeing that they were drawn did she dare to touch the switch. Lamps came on brilliantly; beneath the brightest sat the extension on its own table with a diary and address-book beside it. On this last she pounced and bent over it, leafing with cold hands and uneven movements, now and then throwing hunted glances towards the door. If by some improbable chance Ian had suddenly suspected what she was up to and came after her, she would not hear his footsteps on the thick carpeting. . . .

Ah, here? this must be it . . . ? a cryptic capital C, and under it a number, only one. Something odd struck her, some discrepancy; she was prepared for a squalid succession of numbers struck out, the spoor by which one follows those uneasy creatures addicted to the moonlight flit and to no fixed address. So Paul had described her surely, or had it been Ian . . . ? But no time to think of it now, no time to remember . . .

She glanced at the door again, listened, then with shaking hands picked up the phone. An operator answered and she said composedly, 'Will you give me the address of this private hotel? The number is . . .' and in a few moments had what she wanted as simply as that, with no need of recourse to more elaborate fictions.

She rang off, listened; rose and turned off the lights, listened; cautiously opened the door, listened; in a soundless scurry achieved the first floor, listened . . . not a sound from below, nothing.

When safe in her bedroom, and when undressing, and when in bed, one thought possessed her: *So far I'm ahead of them.* A small strategic advantage since she had as yet no fixed plan of action, no real idea of what she was going to do. But by every probability she had the advantage of time; time was important. Early tomorrow morning Paul would have the address she had just obtained (or pilfered) and present it to his father; in gentlemanly rhythm of action carried on in gentlemen's hours, father and son would foregather with the solicitor before noon; when the conclave had decided which agent to set on Chantal the agent must be interviewed, instructed . . . by that time she would have been long since in and out of Chantal's lodgings, assuming that she found her there. And if not she was defeated, yet she had done her best to warn the girl of the forces arrayed against her—the well-to-do man based on his home territory, pursuing the friendless alien with solvent and resourceful vindictiveness . . .

So far I'm ahead of them, she thought again, *now and tomorrow morning I'm ahead of them,* and evaded the comfortless unwilled postscript, *For all the good it'll do you—or her.*

XI

Her nervousness was perhaps overdone, but defensible. If the girl were living so disreputably that it amounted to a sort of an unofficial prostitution, or among drug-users or similar—first, how would she find her? second, how secure the requisite privacy in a warren overcrowded and perhaps dangerous . . . ? The sight of the house itself was not reassuring, one of a row of five-story portico houses, good-class dwellings only twenty or thirty years ago and now tumbling shamelessly into slums, old filthy paint, scabby patches of fallen-off plaster, battered front doors; all London was riddled with these relics, badly converted and swarming with transients. On this particular example the word CARETAKER on a tarnished plaque seemed wildly optimistic, even if it had not been derided by the old iron bell-pull hanging out by its roots; she pushed tentatively at the door and was unsurprised to find it open. Her first glimpse of the rack of rusty slots beside the door—without bells —at least removed her lingering suspicion that the phone number, and consequently the address, were not Chantal's; in some of the slots were impromptu bits of grimy paper or cardboard, and on one was scrawled *Clarke-Fournier*. All the other names were different, so it was no lurid den of vice, nothing but a cheap letting-house, typical; full of students or low-echelon working-people, an inevitable percentage of them slovenly, dirty or destructive. The large tiled entrance hall, on this late Autumn day, held the customary deathly chill haunted by ancient English ghosts of cabbage and Brussels sprouts, nowadays throttled by lustier alien stinks of garlic and curry. As she passed a huge decayed old sideboard her eye picked up disorderly drifts of circulars and letters, many with exotic stamps and illiterate handwriting. The rack had given no clue to Chantal's whereabouts in this barrack; she must find it herself, and started climbing upward through the house, silent as a tomb. All those employed must have left by now, and possibly Chantal among them; she herself had started for this place the instant that Ian and Paul were gone. The earliest she could manage, but perhaps not early enough. . . .

A radio playing was a welcome sound in the unbroken quiet; timidly she knocked at a closed door and asked the consequent aperture for Miss Fournier, and only vaguely directed resumed her climb. The half-revealed apparition of whiskery face and long tangled hair, momentary as it was, had sent forth a blast of old stale sweat, overpowering. On the second floor rear she confronted three closed doors, listened, thought she detected a stirring behind one of them, and knocked on the gamble. It was opened by Chantal—Chantal no longer in skintight pants and top-heavy with cheap gilt chains and wild hair flying, but neatly combed and dressed in a dark woollen shift without ornament. With face blanked-out, with no identifiable emotion of any kind, she stood regarding her visitor.

'May I come in?' asked Mrs. Milland, and when Chantal stepped aside, unanswering, took it for permission and walked in. The narrow slit of a room contained two narrow cots, a lurching chest of drawers; a narrow aisle between these objects, barely affording passage for one, was covered by a threadbare strip of carpet. With surprise she found her advance expectation of abandoned and degraded sluttishness completely unfulfilled. The beds were smoothly made up, the room and its miserable furnishings austerely, spartanly clean; she thought of the mare's-nest disorder of Chantal's room in her own house, and recognized it belatedly as deliberate provocation. Chantal must have hated her, she thought, startled. But why, why . . . ?

'May I speak to you a moment?' she pursued, at the girl's nod added, 'Could we sit down?' and anticipated permission by establishing herself on one of the cots; she distrusted the look of the single flimsy chair. Chantal, after a momentary hesitation, took the opposite cot, and with half-bent head and downcast eyes—sullen, constrained and defiant all at once—sat waiting. In the moments while Mrs. Milland was thinking how to bridge the abyss, eighteen inches wide and fathoms deep, that lay between them, she was also experiencing a curious sense of awakening and revision. Chantal was a familiar figure to her, certainly, but like a revelation she knew this familiarity as only through the eyes of an angry and cheated employer. The room had a single large window, uncurtained, and by its strong sunless light she saw, as if for the first time, the youth of the girl in the plain dark-blue shift, her clear luminous skin and the thick dark hair that swept back in sculptural lines from her forehead; bare-armed, she seemed not to mind the chill of the barren unheated room. Chantal herself

136

was as brilliantly clean as the room, and all she could think at the moment was, *what a fine healthy girl.* By the same lights, inward and outward, she saw with new eyes the strong straight brows and the large eyes beneath them, the Gallic excellence of feature invincibly founded on aristocratic bone-structure. Stunning, a stunning simplicity; she remembered Chantal's frequent excursions through their front door blatant with unnatural-coloured rouge and lipstick and in get-up so outrageous as to compromise the house from which she issued; another flaunting challenge of some kind, plainly if mysteriously meant as an insult. To herself, who else? To the mistress of the house. . . .

'Chantal,' she began. 'Chantal, you're going to have a baby, and you say it's Paul's?'

A silence from Chantal, rather long, acknowledged this; after it she said, 'Yes,' then slowly, laboriously continued, 'I say it is Paul's, because it is true. I say the truth.'

'Well,' Heather returned practically. 'Very well, if it's true something must be done about it, there's time. But for what I want to tell you—now—there is no time.' She drew a quivering breath. 'No time at all, and you must listen, Chantal, you must believe me and you must be sensible—'

'What is it?' the girl demanded sharply. The strained anxiety that roused her to a straighter posture and made a haggardness in her face, stabbed painfully and responsively in Mrs. Milland's heart. 'You want, yes, to tell me somessing? what? what?'

'Paul has told my husband the child isn't his.' Let her have it quickly and brutally, she thought; the nature of the message allowed of no circumlocution, just as it allowed of no loss of time. 'Well, Mr. Milland has two plans for dealing with the situation. The first is to have a private enquiry agent investigate you, follow you I expect, find out how you live—'

'But you see how I live!' Chantal interrupted harshly, with one of her dramatic outflung gestures. 'You see! And my friend, the ozzer girl—she works, she is *une personne sérieuse*, not a—'

'Yes, yes,' Heather overbore her. 'But in case you happened—once in a while—to associate with people who use drugs, or—'

'But I do not!' Chantal cried. 'I have never, never—'

'Yes, all right, all right, you don't. But in case you did I had to warn you—to be careful. Because you'd be watched and followed and—and reported on. I had to warn you, in case.' She stopped for sheer nervousness. 'That's one of the plans. The other—' again she stopped.

'Yes? yes?' The girl's riveted look upon the other's face was like a force dragging out the words, one by one. 'He plan somessing else for me, yes? . . . What?'

'My husband has an idea you're here illegally.' Again Heather let her have, full, what there was no way around. 'He can find out very easily. And of course you'd be sent back to France straightaway, if he's right.—Don't tell me, don't tell me,' she protested quickly. 'I don't want to know.'

But she knew already, by Chantal's look. Most likely she had outstayed her *Permit to Reside*, a thing happening in hundreds of cases, judging by brief allusions in the public prints. Strange how despair could make a young face old and haggard; she had seen that look in pictures of children in famine areas.

'So you see,' she resumed. 'In case it's true, the best thing you can do is get out of here as quickly as you can, so that the agent can't find you.'

Suddenly an image of dismaying pathos struck her; the hunted creature gathering up its poor bits and pieces and running with them to . . . to where? . . .

'Madame.' Chantal, recalling her, was plainly nailed to some vision of her own; her voice, very low, seemed to distil out of some inward crouching. 'Your husband, he has told Paul he will do all ssiss? He has *told* him?'

'Yes, he told him.'

'And Paul, Paul has said yes? He has said to his father, Yes, do ssiss to her?'

'Y-yes.' No use denying it to the extorting eyes pinned on her. 'Yes, Paul agreed.—Now Chantal.' Briskly she pulled free of her useless acute discomfort. '—there're two other possibilities. And remember, please, please,' she besought, 'these aren't my conditions, it's not I that—that—well.' No time, again, to flounder in search of euphemisms. 'You still won't agree—' with quick and shamefaced furtiveness she canvassed the girl's figure, still flawless '—to an abortion? Or is it too late?'

'Always,' said Chantal without emphasis; the full meaning of it reached Mrs. Milland tardily, after which she had to pick herself up from the feeling of having been knocked flat.

'Well then,' she persisted. 'If you'd agree to—to take money in settlement, I expect that would—would straighten it out so far as—as—' she paused and waited; the girl's silence, ominous, could be prelude to nothing but an explosion of resentment.

'I expect,' she proceeded bravely nevertheless, 'they'd be glad to drop the whole thing if—'

'Paul,' Chantal murmured. 'He has let his father do ssiss to me.'

'I mean—,' she struggled on with embarrassment always deeper and more shaming, seeing what Chantal's silence meant; merely that she had not been listening. '—my husband's prepared to be quite generous, and if you'd write to him straightaway—'

'No,' said Chantal, seeming to return from a distance. Her voice, from low and ominous, had become abstracted. 'No, I will not write.'

'You'd rather hide? run away? Then,' she pointed out ruthlessly, 'you'd better get out of here quickly. At this moment Paul and his father are consulting a solicitor about finding an agent—all that takes time, it'll give you a little time, but not much.'

'Yes,' Chantal agreed, still immeasurably far off. 'Vous avez raison.'

'Now I'm sure you need—' Heather was sliding the strap of her handbag down her arm. 'You—'

'No.' Chantal made an imperious gesture of prohibition. 'No, madame.'

'Now don't be foolish, you—'

'No,' said Chantal. 'It is not necessary.'

'Chantal, look.' Heather was also imperious. 'If you won't —won't go to a clinic or accept a settlement there's only one thing left—you must not be here when the agent comes. A little money, just a little, will make it easier to go away—'

'No,' Chantal interrupted. 'I shall not go away.'

'But what will you do? what will you do, Chantal?'

'*Soyez tranquille, madame,*' Chantal reassured, and rose unhurriedly. 'I know what I shall do.'

'Chantal.' Heather came more slowly to her feet, as if by duress of the other's movement. If this headstrong creature were rejecting the inevitable and contemplating some new aggression it was a fatal idea, in view of the forces drawn up against her. 'Chantal—'

'Why have you come to me like ssiss?' the girl interrupted again, yet always with that strange absentmindedness. 'Why have you done ssiss for me? *Je ne l'ai point merité.*'

'No, you haven't, but it's neither here nor there, I don't know why I came and it's not important. But Chantal, see here, without money you—'

'It is all right, madame.' Chantal's voice—unbelievably —was soothing, her stance dismissive. 'I thank you that you have come to tell me ssiss, I thank you very much.'

Nonplussed with incomprehension and conjecture, Heather gaped at her. By some unlikely alchemy of atmosphere, it was now the younger woman who dominated the elder, and in no small degree. The girl, slightly the taller and beautifully made, stood there with an air of ascendancy, a sort of . . . of grandeur, yet still veiled in her remoteness. . . . Into this distant look, as Heather stared, fell a shadow of something else, stricken; a desolation fleeting as quickly as seen, or turning so soon to hardness that it might have been imagined. But the look that succeeded it, implacable, was no matter of imagination.

'Thank you, madame,' Chantal repeated, and opened the door. 'Thank you so much.'

Ejected by mere spiritual compulsion, Mrs. Milland traversed the grimy odorous stairs and halls, reached the street, and started to walk, a moving target for too many flying arrows of realization; or if not new, never before so directly aimed as to strike so painfully home. *Young,* she thought painfully, *young,* and by illumination of her pain began revising all she had ever heard or felt on the subject of youth. False, she saw now, most of it false; lying formulas and roseate nonsense. Youth the happiest time of one's life? Rubbish, wicked rubbish; youth could be happy under fortunate and understanding influences, but not otherwise. Youth was an open wound, a time of life most open to unhealing hurt, fear or uncertainty; the time of cruellest insecurity and blundering misdirection; the time of being in the hands of others, and defenceless if those hands—however well-meaning—were clumsy, inept, or otherwise unsuitable. Youthful arrogance, hardness and rudeness were masks on young faces, and beneath those masks the inexperience, the ignorance, the rudderless terror . . . Young people, she thought startled, what a lot they endure from their elders, so much of it oppressive or odious but familiar, an order of the day accepted without much feeling or criticism; but looking back upon her own home—upon the atmosphere induced by her father —she felt an unqualified horror. At eighteen or nineteen mere lack of criterion had kept her from being actually unhappy, but not for worlds would she live her youth over again. Neither was Chantal's youth lyrical; at nineteen she was poor and alien in a strange land, pregnant with a fatherless child, an object to be pushed around or pushed out . . . *Thank you so much,* she had said; why should the acquired Anglicism come back to her with such special pathos . . . ?

She passed an old man, shambling along; some beggars begged silently through solicitation of appearance, natural or by cosmetics. But no cosmetic could counterfeit those stiff bowed shoulders and strengthless gait, those thin shoulder-blades almost pushing through the thin old coat. She thrust a coin into his hand and brought away its awful work-hardened feel, leathery and cold and dry, the cushions of the fingers stiff, with little power to open or close. This was the real burden she had brought away from the girl's room, the sense of misery close and actual; the sharp awakening to the human condition. This presence, attending her home, contested her other preoccupation: her unceasing and unsuccessful attempts to reconcile the brazen creature descending the steps, the prime mover of that ugly earlier betrayal, with the girl in the clean, poor, lonely room.

XII

The doorbell's invasion of the Saturday morning was unusual; a ringing not violent but sustained and decided, rousing in her an irritation correspondingly decided; they were ready to drive to the country, their cases stood ready in the hall along with the Fortnum hamper for their hostess. With full-armed readiness to repel she went to answer, only slightly diverted from her wish that she were not involved in this visit to wealthy business friends of Ian's. She knew better, however, than to resist her husband's wish that they should appear in orthodox double-yoke, and was putting her trust in this abnormal November, still dry and mild with hazy sunlight by day and an immense hunter's moon overfull of brilliance at night; if the weather should break suddenly and pen them up in the Lumley's unfamiliar opulence while rain poured down outside, how dreary. . . .

Abrupt and unwelcoming she pulled the door open upon a presentable elderly man, strongly-built, in a heavy-weather mackintosh over a dark suit, and said forbiddingly, 'Yes?'

The man conveyed to her nothing at all; he replied courteously, 'Good morning, madam,' and was holding up a card heavily encased; her momentary impulse to decline inspection of his credentials as some insurance salesman—he had that look—was abruptly displaced by the words that all at once leaped out at her: Detective Inspector . . . his name somehow dim but his title burning out at her, black like pokerwork. Wonder and conjecture flashed through her; some motoring offense? no, not so high an official for that—before the twin currents of fear and premonition fused coldly in her head and rent her with shock.

'Paul . . . ' she gasped; her fainting voice scrabbled against inexorable circumstance like a trapped animal in a corner. 'Paul . . . an accident . . . hurt . . . ?'

'Why no, madam,' returned the man, and his stolidity not only arrested the blackness closing down on her but allowed her to see his palpable surprise. But why, how, what had happened. . . .

'Actually it is Mr. Paul Milland whom I've come to see,' he was continuing. 'And you are Mrs. Milland?'

'Yes, I'm his mother.'

'But from what you say,' he pursued, 'it appears he's not at home—?'

'No,' she managed weakly, then—instead of asking the natural question—actually laughed, in a foolish ecstasy of relief. 'I'm sorry,' she apologized. Her hands had gone icy; she put one against the wall to steady herself. 'But you . . . *frightened* me so!'

'Very sorry,' in turn he uttered apology with no hint of apology in it. 'But will you please tell me where he can be reached? It's extremely urgent.'

'I've no idea,' she began with perfect truth, then halted before his aspect—unsmiling before and now increasingly grim. 'We seldom do know of his plans,' she explained, somehow flurried. 'He's a grown man with a car of his own, and he—'

'May I speak to you?' he cut her off; his manner silenced in advance her protest, *But we're just starting for the country,* or indeed anything else she were inclined to say. Mechanically she answered, 'Please come in,' then turned and preceded him into the living-room, stupid with bewilderment and waiting.

'You mean, Mrs. Milland,' he demanded point-blank, 'that you've literally no idea of his whereabouts? not even whether he's in Sussex, Kent, Essex—?'

'No,' she repeated. 'I'm very sorry, but he—'

'That's all right,' he made short work of her. 'We'll have it on television and radio within the hour. We'll find him.'

'But why, why?' Belatedly her shocked wits coalesced to the point of demand. 'What's wrong? what do you want him for?'

'We want him,' he returned deliberately, 'to help us in our enquiries.' The euphemism, never meaning any good, was prelude; with staring eyes and half-open mouth she could feel her breath suspended, her heart stop beating. 'In regard,' he pursued his unhurried and stately way, 'to a Miss Chantal Fournier.'

'Chantal? But I know her.' Had Ian outreached her after all, raised the hue and cry already . . . ? 'I saw her only a few days ago,' she babbled on. 'Are you sending her back to France? It's a bit cruel, you know, she's only—' it was his hooded look that stopped her all at once, a look never born of mere deportation proceedings, and simultaneously the wave smote her with full towering force. Of course, of course, and she like a fool limping behind events, as usual. . . .

'Has she . . .' she half-whispered, half-moaned, '. . . done something to herself . . . ?'

'Not to herself, madam,' he replied imperturbably.

She stared at him.

'As to how the young woman's condition is regarded,' he continued with calm detachment, 'hospitals won't commit themselves. But this much I may tell you, that we have a policewoman constantly at her bedside. Very considerable weight, as you know, is attached to a dying statement.'

Of all his words, only one remained in her ear. Dying; dying as an actuality, the act of dying, unimaginably applied to that girl so immensely alive; alive in all the vitality of her stance, her thick glossy hair and bare arms, luminous with health and strength. And young, a young creature like that dying? ridiculous, impossible, there was some mistake.

'It's no case of suicide,' dimly his voice penetrated her cotton-wool of rejection. 'And the young woman, so far as she's been able to speak, has definitely involved your son. Not suicide as I say, madam; if she dies it's murder, manslaughter at the very least. By poisoning—something given her by your son, on his insistence that she bring on an abortion.'

Mrs. Milland stood a moment, then started to fall. Not that unconsciousness was releasing her for even a moment, nothing so merciful; it was sickness of shock that cut her legs from under her. Remotely, through swimming nausea, she was conscious of the strong grip on her arm that forced her to sit, then bent her down towards the floor. At once her head started clearing, to accompaniment of his urgent voice, 'Please, madam, we've no time for that. Please—!'

Still upside-down she croaked, 'I'm all right now,' and was helped to sit up. From inner brokenness and dishevelment she regarded him, then managed, 'My husband—I'll call my husband.'

'Yes please,' he acquiesced, distrustfully watching her efforts to rise and obviously ready to catch her again. 'Can you, madam? shall I?'

'No, no, I'll . . .' she almost fell over something; her hat, that had dropped off when she was standing on her head. At the foot of the stairs she held on to the newel-post, and at the third attempt produced a quavering sound, unrecognizable. 'Ian. Ian. Ian.' Over his answering voice, eternities distant, she kept repeating senselessly, 'Come down please. Come down. Come down—'

His appearance at the stairhead, the sight of his wife who stood swaying and supporting herself while keening *Come down, come down,* fired him with the same first alarm and the same first conclusion as her own.

'Paul!' he ejaculated sharply, ran down, and at sight of the stranger demanded, 'Our son?' Even in so brief a moment his colour had gone bad, his voice husky. 'An accident? serious—?'

'Not an accident, sir, not an accident,' the Inspector hastened to reassure. 'The young gentleman's safe and sound presumably, we don't know his whereabouts.—I expect,' he interrupted himself, 'the lady had better sit down—?'

In the living-room, sunk in the chair to which a hand on her elbow had guided her, numbly she listened. Ian, silent, heard the officer, once or twice emitting indefinable sounds.

At mention of the specific charge his furious 'Nonsense!' ripped apart the orderly narrative like a jagged knife. 'Poison!' he overrode the other with fulminating scorn. 'What in hell are you talking about? My son an amateur abortionist on the word of—of what? An alien female vagrant, a prostitute or good as—'

'Sir,' the Inspector put in, and continued imperturbably to oppose the flood with *sir*. 'Sir, the charge is not proven—'

'Proven!' The word was petrol to Ian's fury. 'Why, Paul hasn't even seen the girl in weeks, months! She's lying, it's malice, malicious lies—'

'Sir,' the other repeated, his enormous patience born of a thousand collisions like this one; shouted grief and incredulity, protestation and abuse, bending against him like so many paper arrows. 'Sir, you understand that the charge must be investigated, under the circumstances. The girl's in a room by herself—'

The picture began shaping before her eyes with detail and actuality. The silent form in the hospital bed, the other silent presence beside it with notebook and pencil, waiting, always waiting . . . murder, an alien monster in newspapers and novels but not real . . . yet it was here in the charming room whose charm it turned to dust and ashes; a tangible blackness standing upright among them, as the medieval pestilence had been seen actually walking in the gardens of stricken houses. Above all, a death by poison, evoking the image of the body in agony and convulsed, throwing off terrible corruptions in its struggle to throw off the parent corruptor. . . .

The gathering scream within her was cut off by Ian's voice; its sharpness revived her. Obviously in possession of himself again he was not, like her, fainting with cowardice and rushing to meet disaster; he gave nothing up for lost, thank God, he was preparing to fight. . . .

'Just one moment, Inspector—Burridge? Thank you.' He pushed roughly at his immaculate hair. 'Sorry to've been noisy about this, very sorry.'

'Very natural, sir. The shock—'

'Just let me—' Ian cut off the tactful murmur '—get hold . . . get hold of it . . . Just one moment.'

Courteous, the other waited.

'The girl,' said Ian. 'Dying, did you say? actually dying?'

'Well, sir, hospitals won't usually say till there's no way around it, but she's a very sick girl. The trouble is, you see, that they can't administer specific treatment till they know what the specific—er—foreign substance is.' He paused an instant. 'And the girl can't help them, because she herself doesn't know what she's been given. They've run tests on ejected matter, they've identified stuff commonly used in do-it-yourself abortions, but over and above that . . .' His voice died away; the implication hung on the air unspoken.

'You mean,' Ian picked it up, 'that under cover of this ordinary stuff she's been given something . . . dangerous? Is that what you're saying?'

'It appears so,' the Inspector deprecated.

'By my son?' he challenged with limitless scorn.

'According to the girl, yes.'

In the new sudden stillness, fearfully she picked up her head and stared; feeling in her husband's silence the duplicate of her own horror of comprehension. Paul and his technical accomplishments, his brilliance . . . she saw the remembrance of this dry the words on Ian's lips and check his dismissive contempt.

'All right, Inspector.' With unfamiliar harshness, yet dimly, his voice came to her. 'I know now what I need to know. When you've found my son I'll answer for it that he'll come at once, and that you'll find there's not a word of truth—'

The voices receded as if she were going under an anaesthetic; by the time she realized that Ian had accompanied the officer to the door, he was back.

'D'you know anything about this?' he assailed her. 'Anything whatever?'

She shook her head.

'All right,' he returned savagely. 'Christ! all this over a . . . First thing, cancel this weekend nonsense.' He disappeared into the hall, from which sounds and pauses came to her indistinctly. *My son*, he had said to the officer throughout, not *our son;* MY *son*. . . . By the time he came back, she had managed once more to raise her sunken head and look at him. Again his excellent features gave the effect of shrivelling upon the bone; his face was chalky, his atmosphere that of cataclysm. But not of distraction, she saw; he was not distracted but pointed with purpose, like an arrow.

'I'll get hold of Stebbins,' he said, and again started for the door.

'On Sunday—?' she muttered. 'Closed, his . . . ?'

'I've his home number and his country number,' he snapped. 'What d'you think?'

He vanished once more; the sounds of his various pursuit of the solicitor reached her, this time, not at all. Inertia of disaster engulfed her, a fog half-lifting to reveal unsuspected terrors within it. Paul, for all his boasted management of his life and his cool prevision, trapped in this nightmare; Chantal, in all the splendour of her nineteen years' vitality, struck down and extinguished . . . two separate destructions, the more overwhelming in that she was directly responsible for both. It was her visit to Chantal, her ultimatums officiously if unwillingly transmitted, that must have enraged the girl into attacking Paul with such renewed fury that he had lost his head and attempted this desperate way out; it was she alone who had thrust herself into a situation where she had no business to be, inflaming the girl's already-dangerous sense of injury and—in a word—giving the final push to an avalanche balanced on a knife-edge. If she had kept out of it, kept her mouth shut, perhaps none of it would have happened. Never, never again would she obtrude upon circumstance with her fatal well-meaning that turned trouble into calamity; never again maintain her lethal opinions, for anyone's opinion was better than hers, anyone's . . .

'Stebbins is returning from the country.' Ian was in the living-room again. 'Straightaway. He'd just got there, poor sod.'

Her stricken heart lifted slightly; action of any sort was a hope, or at least not hopelessness.

'Damned fools!' Ian was fulminating under his breath. 'An abortionist—Paul!—'

His courage, she thought gratefully; her husband's courage must be her stay, for she had none of her own.

'He'll be cleared, naturally,' he continued his self-colloquy, from which she knew herself excluded. 'But cleared or not, this sort of dirt sticks. What harm it may do him, God only knows . . .'

Against the background of his muttering she cringed with her own fear that he might find out about her visit to the girl; she had rather die than confess it . . .

'He's getting back as fast as he can.' Again Ian was talking of the solicitor. 'In a couple of hours at most, he thinks. I'm seeing him at his office at half-past one. You stop here.'

'How dare you.' Her answer was as surprising to herself as if an extinct volcano had flamed. 'Of course I'm coming too.'

'And I'm telling you you aren't,' he returned with equal force. 'You'll make another of your priceless bloomers, drop some stupid unnecessary brick, and I'm damned if I'll let you spoil everything.'

'What'll I spoil?' Dimly she registered, between them, a moment unrecognizably barefisted. 'What is it you're afraid I'll say?'

'God knows.' His contempt was undisguised. 'You've only to open your mouth and something damaging comes out. It's a gift.'

'I'm coming with you.' Over and over again he was right, she knew it, yet continued facing him with a dogged obstinancy from some unrealized source. 'I happen to be Paul's mother. And Stebbins will ask to see me sooner or later, you know he will. He'll want to see me.'

The check that this administered to Ian, for a perceptible moment, admitted her argument as inconveniently true.

'Oh, Christ,' he muttered, and turned upon her a scarifying look. 'Come then if you're bound to come, all right. But let me do the talking.' He rounded on her suddenly. 'You'll keep your mouth shut, d'you hear?'

The affront of his tone and manner paralyzed her a moment before she echoed, somehow without resentment, 'Keep my mouth shut? about what?'

He hesitated again with a yet-stronger nuance of indecision, before coming out with it flatly. 'Our defence is going to be that Paul's had nothing to do with that damned little slut for weeks, perhaps months, so obviously her story's rubbish. He hasn't seen her recently.' His stare was intimidating. 'He hasn't seen her at *all*, you understand?'

'But he—' still unready, she groped. 'But he *has* seen her—'

'God.' With clenched teeth Ian appealed to some unavailing deity. 'I knew it.'

'W—what—'

'I knew you'd come in,' he threw at her with abrasive fury, 'with your blethering highmindedness, your feeble-minded, idiotic—' he broke off suddenly and cast aside invective. 'Look. The whole ground and basis of our defence will be that the girl's lying out of whole cloth, that she's totally unreliable and disreputable, an associate of layabouts and worse, an amateur prostitute of no fixed address—'

She has a fixed address. Almost she had said it and just saved herself; her head began turning with the narrowness of her escape.

'—that she's penniless, that she's already tried blackmail or good as to get Paul to marry her—' He broke off again, looking at her strangely. 'What's wrong with you? You're white as a sheet.'

'Nothing, nothing. Tell me—go on, tell—'

'I've told you all of it.' Thank God he was not pursuing— at least for the moment—her look of tell-tale fear.

'It mustn't appear,' he was saying, 'that Paul still continued this . . . association . . . even after you'd got rid of the girl. It—mustn't appear.' His glance impaled her. 'You're not to mention that you found him trying to sneak the girl out of the house. You understand?' he shot at her. 'You understand?'

'But Ian.' Dumfounded, she evoked enough desperate calm

to encircle all possibilities. 'The lawyers will question us about everything, there's no conceivable circumstance they won't go into. If they ask about the length of this—this affair between them—how can we say it's over long since when only a few days ago I myself saw them—'

'You didn't see them,' he cut her off. 'You didn't see anything.'

'But—but—'

'Who's to know? I know, you know, Paul knows, and we won't say. Who knows better?' he challenged inimically. 'Who else?'

'But if they ask me—'

'Let them ask. You slung the girl out weeks ago and since then you've never seen her, let alone in the house,' he pronounced. 'It never happened.'

'You mean—lie about it—?'

'What else? Of course lie.'

'No,' she gasped. 'No.'

'Why not?' he snarled, seeming ready to fly at her throat. 'Why not?'

'I—I—'

'What ails you?' he jeered savagely. 'Scruples?'

'No, no—Ian!' she besought. 'Ian, we've got to be absolutely open, it's our one hope, don't you see? If it comes out later that we're—we're concealing something among the three of us—that I've lied—'

'You could lie for Robina,' he bayed at her, 'but not for your son? For your round-heels of a sister yes, but not for—'

'That's just it,' she broke in wildly. 'Don't you see what it may do to Paul if we suppress something, and it comes out later? Don't you see, don't you see?'

'How'll it come out?' he shouted. 'In this case, how?'

'How did it come out when I lied for Robina?' she fought on. 'I thought I was safe, utterly safe. That's just it, don't you see? No one knows how a lie exposes itself. No one can tell, it's got a life of its own, it comes out—!'

'Now listen to me,' he returned brutally. 'You'll damned well do what I tell you, understand? It's the girl's unsupported word, and who'll believe the little slut against the three of us? She's never been in this house since you dismissed her,' he trampled her down, each word iron-shod. 'If the question comes up you'll deny it, that's all, you'll simply deny—'

'No!' she wailed. 'I daren't, I daren't!' Some additional strand in her broke. 'I—I'm *afraid*—!'

The keening, craven admission made a long silence between them, an interval exhausted and empty. After some moments he stirred from an unnatural stillness, and the movement restored sight to her sightless eyes. Something was happening to him, a sort of emergence from access of transport; he was like a person recovering from delirium. Herself little more than a shell, she understood nevertheless how totally shock had unseated him that he could repudiate what his better judgment must surely have told him—that nothing could serve them in this pass but truth, merciless truth. . . .

'All right,' he said, patently not to her. He was ravaged, his eyes sunken, his comely shoulders bowed and bent. 'Better not maybe, we might be taking a chance at that . . .' His glance and his voice returned to her simultaneously; he looked at her full. 'All right,' he pronounced, like doom. 'We'll do it your way, we won't keep anything back. But if it turns out that things go badly because of your interference—because we've done as you insisted—' his voice deepened, his buried eyes never moved from her '—there's nothing more between us, it's the end.'

Her punished head bent lower, acquiescing.

'Nothing now but wait for Stebbins,' he said, again not to her. 'What time is it? Christ, two hours to kill.'

XIII

Strange, the Saturday afternoon vacuum of this part of London, its roaring channels of traffic—solidly packed on weekdays—empty, High Holborn empty; Staple Inn, almost sole survivor of the Fire of London, sadder and darker in its ancientry than usual; it had seen worse troubles than the troubles of the Milland family. Ian parked the car in a solitude, and they walked through the passage to Gray's Inn, the huge garden silent, the old houses silent, and into the particular house where Mr. Stebbins, good enough to return at speed, was awaiting them.

Against all expectation it was a steadying thing to sit in this large old room whose big windows looked out on wide tranquil grass and trees and sunlight; another beautiful day in the phenomenal run of weather they were having. Steadying also to talk to this man, rather dry, immensely dispassionate, not torn by love, not crippled and disabled by fear for someone loved. . . .

158

Otherwise, unreality possessed her; the unreality that instead of approaching the windmill near Biggin Hill in the mild Autumn sunshine they sat in the weekend desertion of an Inn of Court discussing the defence of their son on a possible charge of murder by poisoning; the unreality that made her see and hear other presences as if at one remove. All the same, as Ian did the talking and she let him talk, one compartment of her mind remained awake and alert, ready to interpose at the first hint of evasion, palliation, dissembling. Otherwise nothing remained to her, no perception of time, nothing . . . and the phone bell that shredded apart the two men's discussion shredded her nerves, mercifully anaesthetized, with agonizing recall.

'I connected up when I came,' Stebbins explained with modest pride, reaching. 'It's as much as I know of a panel, but useful.' He replied, giving the number, listened a moment with a shade of surprise, then extended the instrument. 'For you, Mrs. Milland.'

'Paul's back,' said Ian sharply. 'They'd not know where to find us otherwise.'

'But—for me?' She gaped at him. 'You're sure?'

'Mrs. Milland,' he repeated, and as she took the phone, 'Mrs. Milland?' another voice confirmed positively.

'Y-yes.'

'Inspector Burridge here. The girl wants to see you,' he said rapidly. 'Miss Fournier—she's asking for you.'

'Yes,' she returned numbly. Damp sweat broke out on her, a clinging of funeral cere-clothes.

'Please come now,' he was saying. 'At once.'

'Yes. My husband'll drive—'

'A car's on its way,' he interrupted. 'It's there by now, or any moment.'

And indeed as she rang off she could see through the window an archway to the left, and a uniformed figure walking smartly out of it.

The Inspector and a doctor, his upper half in a white tunic, waited in the first floor corridor. Their look, as she approached them . . . a portent? At any moment now? already . . . ?

'Mrs. Milland.' Rapidly, in a low voice, the Inspector bypassed the enquiry of her eyes, of her lips parted but afraid to ask. 'Get her to talk as much as you can. Not too many questions, but encourage her with sympathy and so forth, you know—'

'But if she's . . . if she's actually . . .'

'Have to try,' shrugged the doctor. A forbidding quality in his face and voice was joined to some intense reservation of manner. 'Something funny there,' he added, shrugging again, then snapped his mouth shut. He was quite young, objectionably hard and brusque; one of the new crop, without the courtesy and humanity of the old, and she cared for him not at all.

'Actually,' Burridge supplemented, 'they've thought she was able to talk some hours ago, but she wouldn't—not a word out of her, till she asked for you. Now Mrs. Milland,' he proceeded urgently, 'just very gently and without pressing her, as we've said, try to find out just when she was given this stuff by your son and under what duress, what threats and so forth. If she wants to talk let her talk, don't be nervous about it, a nurse'll be timing her outside—she won't be allowed to overdo it. And the policewoman'll be in the room itself, taking it all down. One thing,' he added rapidly. 'If her voice is too faint, repeat clearly what you've heard and then say, *Is that right?* so it can be recorded. It's not how we'd like it, but it's the best we can do.' On his note of dissatisfaction they paused, having been walking slowly all the while; he indicated a closed door still some feet distant. 'In there.'

The turning of the knob was soundless, her passage over the threshold soundless; just within the door a big three-leaved screen completely blocked any further view, and within the screen a motionless dark-blue uniform sitting with notebook and pencil at the ready, did not even raise its eyes as she passed.

The hush of the room struck first, a hush unlike any other, into which the faint accent of the world outside penetrated as something forever apart and meaningless. In this cubicle containing the imminent event there overwhelmed and subjugated her the sense of that presence to whom human acceptance or rejection are nothing; *the Very and invisible thing,* came to her in chilling misquotation. The moment she stepped clear of the screen she was almost at the bedside, the room being little more than a slit; between the screen and the bed could just be squeezed one small chair. Until seating herself on this she had not even dared look at what lay on the bed; better sustain, sitting, the shock of impending dissolution. The single window, heavily shaded, admitted less a suffusion of light than a suffusion of dimness.

Bending like a suppliant toward the bed, Mrs. Milland summoned her courage and snatched one shrinking glance, instantly withdrawn. Her annihilated gaze brought away an image of prostration, the girl lying at full length on her back, a shape whose sculptural perfection even the threnody of twilight and hospital bedclothes could not dissimulate; about this shape hovered something already transfigured, not of earth. Only no time to think of that, no time. . . .

'Chantal,' she ventured, hardly daring and longing to weep. 'You wanted to speak to me?'

After a moment, something stirred in the pale indistinct face; slowly the head on the pillow turned toward her, slowly the eyes opened.

'Madame,' the girl whispered, and seemed to call on her strength. 'Thank you, madame—that you have come to see me.'

'I wanted to come.' With all her heartbreak, cautiously she pitched her voice a tone higher, mindful of the recorder behind the screen; the louder sound was sacrilege in this enclave of tragedy, but she could not help it. 'I wanted to come because you wanted me to come.'

'Yes,' Chantal whispered. 'Yes.'

Then another pause, long—too long; Heather, through her devastation of pity, yet was equally devastated with a sense of time wasting, wasting, and no enlightenment in it, nothing of help to Paul, nothing of harm either, Oh God let there be some help. . . . Yet how harass the dying, how detain the soul in its passing with human demand and exaction, the creature in—how did it go—*in articulo mortis, in extremis.* The article of death, the extremity; how surpassing the Church's vocabulary for such occasions . . . She cursed her wandering irrelevance in such a moment, and took her courage in both hands.

You wanted to speak to me? she intended saying; with lips already parted, all at once she felt an inward check, tan-

162

gible as if a hand had been clapped over her mouth. Struck motionless in her attitude of petition, within her there passed a strange sequence of gropings, alertings, formless distrust. . . .

Blind, her first entrance into this room; the entrance of a woman with eyes bandaged by culpability, by the knowledge of her son's share in this young mutilated life, by the sense of racking torment undergone, by the sense of approaching fatality . . . all this clouding her power of assessment even more than the dimness of the room her unadjusted eyes. Now with spiritual and physical vision given time to clear she stared as at something—till this moment—totally invisible. Chantal lay once more in profile; pure, severe, aloof, she rested motionless as an effigy on a tomb, her luminous pallor unbroken but for the strokes of thick eyelashes and arched eyebrows, dark opposing crescents.

What continued strengthening within Mrs. Milland, as she gazed, was as powerful as unforeseen. The young young thing struck down in all the pathos of her beauty . . . too beautiful, that was the trouble; it was precisely this elegaic marble perfection that was withering her endless compassion, her longing to make amends, and replacing it with the most extraordinary caution and reserve.

'Chantal,' she repeated, the distrust in her producing a tone much firmer than she had used previously. 'You wanted to tell me something?'

The eyelashes moved again, the head turned toward her once more; again came the slow, fading whisper, 'Madame . . .'

'Louder, could you?' Heather asked; unthinkable demand ten seconds ago, but this was ten seconds later, and in Chantal's face was something that might reasonably be called surprise. 'A little louder—so I can hear?'

'Madame,' Chantal besought, in a voice decidedly more audible. 'He did not give me money—Monsieur McVeigh. He offered, yes, but I have said no, no—'

'Chantal—'

'—I have not had from him one penny. Madame,' she begged in a failing voice. 'For what I have done to you, please will you forgive me?'

'I've forgotten about it, it's all over.' Was this all, she thought frantically, all the girl had wanted to tell her? And what use, what use. . . . 'I forgive you *de tout coeur.*' What if the nurse should enter to say her time was up, and nothing new had been said, nothing of consequence . . .

And with these deathly misgivings there hardened in her, all the time, the thing she was still ashamed to acknowledge wholeheartedly. Mrs. Milland was by no means a stranger to death; she had seen two persons die, one whom she had loved and another she had loved by conventional obligation. In each instance she had seen the same things, the hallmarks of death —the aura of impending evanishment, the fluttering breath, the bridge of the nose and the wrists going sharp and translucent, charged with the same meaning as the sunken flanks of an animal dying. In this moment, looking for all or any of these things, her eyes found none of them—her untrained eyes, she reminded herself. Nevertheless. . . .

'Chantal,' she essayed again, from mere desperation. 'Was that—about Mr. McVeigh—all you wanted to tell me? Was there nothing else?'

'Ah yes,' sighed the girl, 'yes,' and fell again into silence, that racking and maddening silence. . . .

'If you want,' Mrs. Milland persisted, out of her torment. 'If you want, tell me.' Insistence, possibly dangerous, yet what else was there for it . . . 'If you tell me,' she besought, 'you may feel better.'

'No,' murmured Chantal. 'To feel better is not for me, ever.'

Again Mrs. Milland waited with consuming despair and impatience, with dying hope; inwardly fretted to rags but her outward calm intact. What if she were wrong after all, what right had she to be sceptical, what did she really know of death, of signs and symptoms. . . .

'Madame,' said Chantal, and at her inflection every nerve in Heather's body jumped. *Now*, she thought breathlessly, *it's coming now*. To help Paul? to help destroy him? . . .

'Madame,' the pale effigy was continuing, her voice hardly more than an indrawing of breath, 'I lied.'

'I can't hear you,' Heather protested heroically, against the blinding flash of hope and unbelief. 'I can't hear you at all.'

'I lied,' Chantal repeated; her tone rose perceptibly above its first expiring nuance. 'Paul did not give me anyssing, I have not seen Paul for days. I did it myself, only myself, *j'ai voulu me suicider*, I have wished to die. . . .'

As the murmur fell to nothingness Heather offered, 'Thank you, Chantal, for telling me.' Her heart that had weighed a ton suddenly sprouted wings and flew. 'Now tell me what you took. Tell me so they can help you.'

'No,' said Chantal. 'I am ashamed, I will not live ashamed.'

'Tell me,' Heather urged on a note surprisingly peremptory, and Chantal seemed to give up all at once.

'I took the epsom salt,' she vouchsafed, 'and some aspirins what are left in a bottle—'

'They know about that,' said Mrs. Milland factually. 'What else?'

'Some little mustard. Oh, so sick it has made me, sick to die, I am glad to die, glad—'

'Oh no, Chantal,' said Mrs. Milland, with gentlest cruelty. 'I don't expect you'll die.'

The doctor, barely containing his rage, let go without constraint when they were still too near the door.

'That bitch!' he exploded. 'That lying, acting, bloody little bitch! Christ, the tests we've run on her, twenty or thirty of 'em, and you think that costs nothing? Money slung in the gutter, Christ! if I could flay her bottom the way it deserves to be flayed—!'

'But the tests,' the Inspector argued. 'Couldn't you tell, from what they showed—'

'Hell, we were looking,' the doctor flung back in a whisper like escaping steam, 'for something to explain the pain she seemed to be in. You laymen,' he denounced bitterly, 'with your loose assumptions that there're tests for every known poison! Well, there aren't, let me tell you. There're poisons for which there're no known tests at all—poisons that analysis can't recover because they've been broken down in the body—new poisons from new syntheses, still unidentifiable—also we'd been given a hint that a man with technical knowledge was involved. And the girl's symptoms, the faked agony, such a performance you never—'

'And it took you in,' the Inspector commented. 'Trained people like you, doctors—'

'Did you ever hear,' the other hissed violently, 'of simulated or fake symptoms that turn genuine under malingering

166

or violent hysteria? And on top of it the pregnancy compli-
cating everything, making us sweat blood, God what a mess!
We daren't let her abort, we daren't induce it either, with one
or the other she might die. A damned shame she—' he clamped
his teeth shut on what was clearly an unprofessional sentiment
and jerked his tunic straight. 'Well, I should be in about ten
other places this moment.'

'But her present condition,' the Inspector urged. 'How
soon—'

'A few days, and damned few,' the other returned. 'We'll
turn her out of that private room and into a ward at the double, and get rid of her as soon as we can, no fear.'

'You mean she'll recover entirely? she'll—?'

'Recover!' the disciple of Aesculapius cut him off again.
'Why, her contortions didn't even budge the baby, and what
went into her came up so quickly there shouldn't be any harm
that way either. Strong as a horse, that one, she'll be better
than new.' In the act of swinging about he checked, and delivered a missile of final, concentrated virulence. 'For what
that's worth.'

XIV

After an earthquake one saw pitiable pictures of searchers in the ruins; people trying to find bits and pieces of their former lives. And for all that every exterior appurtenance of Mrs. Milland and her husband and son survived unchanged, she at least had the sense of being left knee-deep in ruined fragments where she groped blindly, trying to put her hand on something familiar. *Nothing's the same,* she thought constantly, with the loser's resigned acceptance. *None of us is the same. How can we be, with all that's happened?* Of this family transformation not all was plain to her, only parts of it—as for example the change in Ian and her comprehension of this change, unwanted but complete. There were things people could not bear to see and should not have to see, and one of them she had been forced to see. Nakedness of any kind was in great part unacceptable, and just as naked fear, naked cruelty or naked greed were horrors, so naked love could be scarcely less a horror. She had seen her husband stripped to the bone under the threat of mortal danger to his son; she had seen what his cool and imperturbable façade hid so completely, his helpless absorbed love for Paul, too much, too terrible . . . that he like herself should carry away marks of the encounter was natural and inevitable, these inward scars seeming to manifest themselves in prolonged silences that amounted to brooding—and this in a man who had always condemned silence, in the company of others, as an unpardonable social gaucherie.

With Paul the aftermath was different—or at any rate had begun differently. Paul's immediate response to the episode had been extreme amusement if not flippancy; a disposition to regard it all as an adventure and not even to regret his spoiled weekend. The pursuit by telecast that cornered him sensationally in a country pub had produced the most thrilling excitement, hilarity and suspense in his party of gay young friends, among whom a conquering hero's return undoubtedly awaited him; his mother suspected that only some awkward ingredients in the story would prevent his dining out on it for months afterward. With suppressed reservations and discomforts therefore she was glad, glad that he was untouched; that herself and Ian had sustained the first nightmare impact of a crisis that was over almost before he knew of it.

Yet all the same, and of late, it must be the constraint between his parents that was pushing him more and more into aloofness. Thank God he knew nothing of the wretched and degrading scene that had preceded the visit to Gray's Inn, but he felt something wrong between them; he could scarcely avoid feeling it. She was sorry to see their lingering oppressions infect and subdue him so perceptibly, sorry to see him fall into silences of his own, uncharacteristic. Either way, she could do nothing about it. The dust would settle in its own good time, the rubble be cleared away. *We'll all have to get over it*, she thought dispassionately. *We shall do, of course.* The unbidden voice she so resented added a gratuitous supplement: *More or less.*

'She's got away, that slut,' said her husband, without preamble. 'Disappeared.'

Though days had elapsed without reference of any kind to Chantal, Mrs. Milland's glance and her attention rose from her book, fully engaged.

'What do you mean, disappeared?' she echoed.

'I mean,' he returned in the peculiarly soft voice of his nastier humours, 'in the usual sense of the word. Disappeared from hospital before she was due to go. Got clear away.'

She kept a listening face turned toward him, thankful that he could know nothing of her latest ruinous compulsion: her anonymous call to St. Hylda's as to the girl's situation after discharge, the impersonal voice that first enquired as to her right of relationship or other right to ask, then reared its barrier of courteous formula, that the information was not available. And she had taken the rebuff with gratitude; she had made the gesture, no one could do more, she was now relieved from further concern . . . and here was the girl, a troubling spirit that could not be laid, haunting her again through this new channel. . . .

'When was this?' she asked.

'Three days ago. They've no idea how she did it—not even at what time, exactly.'

'Oh?'

'It's a huge place, overcrowded and understaffed. All the

same, she couldn't have walked out in a dressing-gown and slippers without being noticed,' he pursued. 'She had help, of course—her kind clot together.'

A pause stretched out between them.

'Just when I'd got the Emigration and Labour people interested and on the lookout—for the date of her discharge,' he continued in the musing tone that was half-soliloquy. 'Had it all laid on, then she slips between our fingers—!'

With no word or opinion to offer, she was silent.

'I'll find her,' he was murmuring. 'I shan't stop till I do find her.'

'You've an agent asking—still?' she returned, startled.

'She's not getting away scot-free after all she's done.' His very low voice went well with his very faint smile. 'It's a matter of persevering, after all she can't evaporate. Women like that,' he pursued softly, 'used to be whipped at the cart's tail. And there's a good bit to be said for the custom, you know?'

So this had been the secret of his recent withdrawn silence; not silence of moodiness but silence of waiting; the hunter waiting in ambush for the nineteen-year-old quarry. And the sight, to his wife, was a further revelation of her blindness. She could be married to him for twenty-six years without beginning to realize his feeling for Paul till she had seen it topple him off base and send him snatching at desperate fabrications to shield, at any cost, the object of his love. And just as she had failed to realize his capacity for single-minded and obsessing love, so she was equally behindhand in realizing this other capacity, fixed and changeless, that possessed him to the marrow of his bones.

Don't be surprised at the postmark, the letter began. *No use breaking it gradually, I've taken off with really a very decent sort of bloke, I mean decent as men go. If you knew what it means to've got away from that legal monstrosity of mine, I expect I'd have knifed him one day actually, or jumped off the P.O. tower. The new boy is terribly well-heeled and* VERY *generous, and believe me I'm taking all I can get and asking for more, do you remember how I* HATED *taking anything from anybody. Well, balls to pop-eyed innocence, I'm making hay and tucking it away neatly against the inevitable cold wind etc. He's really not bad, this one, perhaps a bit of a bore and rather silly but so good-natured and kind, Oh God what a change, and anxious to please me, also w.a.c. At the moment I don't know just what we'll do, we shan't stop in Paris, too noisy and spoiled like every other big city. I loathe the plages, all those bodies ugh and the smell of suntan oil double-ugh, and sand in your hair and down your neck. I expect we'll take a country house outside of Paris, but listen, darling, Mrs. C. L. Nichols Poste Restante Paris will find me always, I'll drop in every so often in hopes. If you want to see me (why should you, the beast I've been and all) you'll have to come he-yah because obviously I can't go they-ah. And if Ian's along, you come and meet me alone, do you hear,* ALONE, *I don't want dear Ian looking down his nose at his s-i-l living in sin, the hell with him, smug bastard. Write me as soon as you can or want to and* DON'T LECTURE. *It's all a waste I know, a waste and a mess, but it's too late to do anything about it. Charlie seems frightfully keen and would marry me like a shot if I had my divorce, but in the circumstances H. will never give me one, bless him. Darling Hezzer, much much much love.*

Pss Wouldn't it be a Charlie, just my luck.

Mrs. Milland lowered the letter with a faint smile; Robina somewhere in distance was better than no Robina at all. The smile, too small and uncertain to prosper in life, passed away and became a look of active but unconvinced calculation. Immediate prospect of France there was none, neither with Ian nor alone. She might of course, by dint of vigorous and sustained attack, go over on her own . . . fury rose in her, a sudden nausea of revulsion. Why must so modest an objective as a few days' trip to Paris be a matter of such hesitations, such struggle and scheming? And with the thought a knowledge broke over her, the tidal wave of a drowning finality. Struggle and scheming, initiative and energy, were once and for all beyond her. Some mainspring in her was broken, not only of purpose but of desire. She was empty and tired to death; bankrupt in the literal sense of the word, finished.

And in any case, dear as Robina was, she had preoccupations more immediate and more pressing. Such as the formless thing that had beset her on hearing of Chantal's escape from hospital, the thing she had been only too willing to dismiss as imagination, and that now—by some ominous momentum within itself—had gathered outline, substance, and the heart-stopping quality of a weight suspended on a fraying thread; overhanging not her, not Ian, but the one person most important on earth to both of them.

Paul, she kept thinking, *Paul,* as if repeating his name could ward off an approaching evil, like an incantation; moreover, to ignore this relentless sense of something imminent was—she knew by instinct—merely to bury her head in the sand.

If Chantal's baby were his, and her conviction of this survived unshaken, he had done a cruel, cowardly and despicable thing. And this sort of wrong she saw now—with new and frightening clarity—as a lie of action, just as the spoken untruth was a lie of speech. And by the inner and organic law of falsehood—its unpredictable life-span that made it a debtor calling in some unknown future to collect compound interest—this debtor must, sooner or later, call upon Paul. Chantal was not one to lie down under the treatment she had received if she knew anything about her; she was heavy not only with child but with grievance, a menace biding its time. Remembering the girl in all her quality of native force, it was easy to imagine her with a knife in her hand, or gun, or bottle of acid. Or again, her successful escape from hospital must mean she had friends who helped her and who might champion her cause. Egged on by Chantal, how easily such champions might administer a beating to Paul with coshes or kickings, leaving him to be found in some alley, hurt physically and perhaps mentally . . . in a sort of nightmare swoon she saw him, in all his accomplishment and brilliance of mind, broken and destroyed, an imbecile. . . .

She would drive the frightful vision away by assuring herself that Paul was lucky, that by luck—which made nothing of the most remorseless logic—he had got away with his lies of speech and performance; slipping free of their penalties, exempt . . . yet why should Paul be exempt, more than another? Why should the law of events set in motion by the lie, be suspended for his special benefit? Then again she invoked the talisman of his luck, in the same blind spirit by which—even at this time of her life—she averted her head when passing a country graveyard at night; sickening alternations of justifiable fear and unjustifiable self-deception . . .

Nor was comfort to be found in the latest phenomenon, the aspect of Paul himself. He was different, undoubtedly different, and it seemed to her that this change had taken place in him before she had begun to notice. Through distorting lenses of anxiety she began watching him—covertly, so as not to risk his notice or resentment. His silences, that she had ascribed to oppressive parental atmosphere, had darkened into something she could describe in only one way —the look of a man with something hanging over him. Perhaps (her heart contracted) perhaps he had already been threatened? through warning notes or anonymous phone-calls, or like intimations that he was not yet done with Chantal, or rather that Chantal was not yet done with him? In that case she and Ian would hear nothing about it; by a male convention completely understandable to her he could ask his parents' help and advice against matrimonial entrapment, but not against physical intimidation; there he must fend for himself as he judged best, with such means as he had. Nor dared she question him, get it out of him; another of her ill-starred interferences might make everything worse, she had learned her lesson. To live ground between the upper and nether millstones of her fear, and her fear of doing nothing about her fear, was a new lesson she had to learn. Another and harder lesson was to see Paul carrying the burden that permitted of no sharing, and to know that in her resided no virtue of support or help unless he chose to speak; and even if he spoke, perhaps not then.

XV

The sound of a key in the lock—before three of a weekday afternoon—was enough to bring her to the head of the stairs, and the sight of Paul at such an hour enough to make her descend rapidly.

'Darling?' she began in general enquiry, then came to a sudden halt—of confused alarm, of premonition that his trouble had become too much for him alone, that he was coming to her with it—

'Mummy,' he interrupted, before she could speak further. 'You've got to help me.'

'Yes,' she returned, keyed up in every fibre with the need to serve him. 'Of course.'

'Let's sit down and talk.' Taking her elbow and propelling her towards the living-room, in turn he halted suddenly. 'Is she anywhere in the house—Mrs. Amin?'

'Never after two,' she replied, and let him half-push her along with more urgency than he was aware of.

'Mummy,' he began, the moment they were seated. 'Look,

there's no use waffling about it, I'll get it off my chest straight-away and we can fight about it later. Chantal and I are marrying tomorrow, I've got it all laid on, it's going to happen and that's that. Now go ahead and get it off *your* chest if you like, but nothing you say's going to make things any different.'

After a moment—

'I shan't say anything,' she returned, understanding why he assumed disapproval and resistance from her; after all he had no knowledge of her battles with Ian on the score of Chantal.

'Well, I'm glad you aren't going to tear strips off me,' he acknowledged frankly, 'because it wouldn't have done any good. But look, Mummy, there're—I mean—there're things about this that—I mean, they're going to be pretty damned awkward for me. Not nice at all, in fact decidedly nasty.'

He paused, mustering a statement of probabilities that she knew, in advance, more comprehensively than he could ever know them.

'Father's got it in for Chantal,' he pursued. 'I mean, hot and heavy, I've never seen him like this. Of course he's down on her for that hospital business and dragging in the cops, I understand that, but it's all he's got against her. And if I'm not taking it all that hard, why should he? He is though, he's fairly gone overboard—' nonplussed, he shrugged gloomily. 'You know how he's always been, never feels all that strongly about anything, nothing's worth it. But he hates her, Mummy, he actually hates her. By the little he's let out now and then, I've realized how much he's been keeping inside.'

He paused again, giving his mother a first sight of her elegant and self-sufficient son as a thoroughly unhappy young man.

'Well,' he launched himself again, on a gusty exhalation. 'If I just waited till he comes home this evening, and faced him with it—just let him have it—you can imagine what'll happen. A bloody awful row, so stinking and rotten that we—well, we'll never be friends again. Hell, I don't want that to happen.'

Now his look was undisguisedly wretched; she had a renewed and powerful sense of his bond with Ian, and realized again the disturbing and pathetic sight of love laid bare.

'So I was wondering—' he laboured on, with petition also naked '—if you'd—well—break it to him first, sort of prepare the—the ground—before I talk to him, I mean—would you?'

'I—I'll try.'

Some hint of her inward quailing must have come through to him; quickly he besought, 'I know it's a stinking trick, letting you in for the first blast, but I—well, if I simply put it to him, take it or leave it, there'll be a . . . red-hot bust-up or an ice-cold bust-up, and either way—' he shrugged '—it's the end. So I'm hiding behind Mummy like a little hero, I'm funking it—no use calling it anything else.' He pulled out an immaculate handkerchief and mopped his forehead.

'I'll do what I can,' she promised bleakly.

'I'm a louse,' he embroidered the theme. 'But I've had practise.' His eyes left some inner vista and returned to her. 'It's all I've been through the whole business, a louse. Chantal. . . .'

He stopped abruptly, then paused for so long that the prospect of dealing with Ian had time to loosen its paralyzing

grip on her, and reshape itself about Paul. He was going to
say something important; she listened hungrily.

'I want you to know all about it,' he blurted, and the words
—for all the circumstances—somehow touched her with a
life-giving warmth.

'If I can come crawling and ask you to put in a word for
me,' he was pursuing, 'I expect I owe you that much.'

'You owe me nothing,' she murmured sadly; he had spoiled
it.

'No, no, I don't mean like that, by way of barter,' he protested quickly. 'You're the one I want to tell it to, that's all
I mean, only you.'

She nodded, the warmth reviving faintly.

'It's all so damned mixed-up,' he was complaining, trying
once more to lay hands on the free end of some intricate
snarl. 'You do a rotten thing and you go on doing it, you know
better but you just . . . I was being the devil of a fellow,
I expect, the Casanova of Chelsea.' His mouth shaped to a
bad taste. 'She—Chantal—she held out for a while, there's
something peculiar in her background, something she'd never
tell me—and I thought she'd had some experience, a gor-
geous bit like that, but she hadn't had—and when she gave
in, she went completely overboard. Well, that part of it . . . '
a new thing was in his eyes, a reflected light ' . . . I expect
it'll never happen to me again, and if I live to be a hundred
I'll be glad I had it.'

He paused again, remote but certainly not embarrassed,
and by some communicated flash she could guess at something of unknown dimension—something quite unlike her
own concentration of love, garlanded with social approval

179

and the bright wedding-day and the country church, adorned and beflowered.

'Well, and then—it began to scare me, there was something about the way she felt, too much . . . I saw I'd taken on more than I'd bargained for, and I didn't want . . . or I wanted it, yes, but I didn't want it. It was too much,' he repeated. 'And I began looking for a way out.' His eyes became direct and met hers. 'Anything would do, any dodge so I could free myself, that's the size of it. And yet—crazy about her all the time—it wasn't comfortable.' He drew a labouring breath. 'Well, and then she was in pod. And didn't demand marriage, mind you, just took for granted nothing else was possible, in this lofty way—she can be pretty damned lofty.'

Yes, she assented silently, remembering the ascendancy that had turned her out of the poor bare room; lofty was the word.

'And it was that I expect, her assuming it so coolly, that turned me up.' He looked sheepish. 'I wasn't being pushed into anything I didn't want, I didn't fancy my neck in a noose, and I said no. And that turned her into a fury, then my suggesting she get rid of it turned her completely . . . elemental . . . and I got angry and began hating her and wanting to hurt her—and not being able to stop loving her all the same, God,' he groaned, 'what a mess. Then little Paul got a bright idea.'

He stopped dead a moment.

'Play it cool, do the frank boyish bit and let Papa handle it. I knew he'd pull me out of it—against him, she'd have no chance. And I knew he'd assume straightaway that she was promiscuous, lazy, on drugs, the lot, he'd assume everything I wanted him to assume. All I had to do was lie—by keeping my mouth shut. Well, that's . . . ' he swallowed. 'I haven't explained it very well but that's how it was. Sort of.'

'Yes,' she murmured, into another pause. 'Yes, darling.' 'I did a stinking thing.' It was doubtful if he had heard her. 'I crawl when I think of it, and I think of it all the time. You can't live with yourself on those terms day after day, you can't do it.' With one of those alternations between soliloquy and confession, he looked at her again. 'So I tucked her into a nice little hotel in Bayswater—after I'd whipped her away from the hospital.'

'How—' against all the trouble impending, she was curious '—how did you do it?'

'Easily. I got that friend of hers, that Daphne Clarke, to take her a note about what I'd planned. And as soon as she was on her feet, Daphne just brought her a coat and hat and shoes to the patients' lounge—it's a scruffy little hole, not much used—and stood at the door while she put them on, then the two of them just walked out together.'

'But how—how did you know where to find Daphne—' she checked, with sudden and full comprehension. 'So you did know her address all the time,' she observed neutrally. 'You told Ian she had none, that she floated about and you could only reach her by—'

'I know.' He blushed, a phenomenon she had not seen since his boyhood. 'I had to pretend not to know it, I had to make father think she slept here and there. Another DSO for Milland. And I—I—' he was stammering, an occurrence equally unknown. 'I faked her a recommendation to get her in here—had someone else write it, in case you knew my fist.' He blushed a deeper red. 'No, she's never had but the one address—the same bedsit with the same girl. The whole dodge was my idea entirely, I put her up to it. So—' his voice hardened against the opposition he still expected from her '—that's that.'

'I . . .' she hazarded, after a silence '. . . I was only wondering . . .'

'Yes?'

'—well, all this—this upset and bitterness that's been between you and her—you haven't come out of it with too much against each other?'

'I've got no more against her than she's got against me,' he returned with decision. 'Not nearly so much.'

'Well,' she said meekly. 'So long as it hasn't spoiled things between the two of you—'

He started to speak, then checked visibly, frowning.

'It's—it's knocked off some of the gilt, I expect.' He was thoughtful but forthcoming. 'But the gilt's the least of my worries. It gets knocked off later in any marriage, doesn't it? So just as well sooner as later, perhaps?'

'Perhaps.'

'Actually, I could go the hell of a lot farther and fare worse. I reckon she's as good a chance of happiness as I'm likely to get. As far as bed goes, it could hardly be better.'

'I see,' she murmured, skirting around a frankness forever not for people of her generation.

'But don't think I'm marrying her for that,' at once he contested the withdrawal in her voice that she had been unable to prevent. 'And I'm not doing it out of guilt or chivalry or that rot, I'm doing it because—'

Again he stopped suddenly, and again like a person faced

182

with the necessity, through unavoidable crisis, with unavoidable definition.

'—because—well, actually—' he spoke slowly at first; then decisively, having found words. 'I lied like a rat and she lied like a bitch. We both lied, we both made a bad mistake and the best we can do is—is help—help each other get out of it and—and get over it. And the funny thing is—' with growing bafflement he fought the shortcomings of definition '—she's the only one that can help me and I'm the only one that can help her. It's funny but that's how it—Oh hell, I'm making a mess of it.' He gazed at her with frustration. 'But I can't put it any better than that.'

'No, no, it's all right, I—I see.'

'Actually, Mummy, you've no idea of what she—what she's like.' He was pathetically anxious. 'Even when we were going strongest she'd never take anything from me, no help of any kind, no presents, nothing. Well, after the kind one sees mostly—greedy—you've got to admire that sort of thing. Actually when you know Chantal, you've *got* to admire her. I mean, I can't imagine her doing anything that isn't absolutely straight, she's—well—terrifically honest—' he broke off, his look eloquent of appeal and inadequacy.

'Yes, dearest, yes,' she hastened to fill the gap; his propitiation, and the absurdly young look it gave him, touched her painfully. 'Yes, I'll speak to your father, I'll do my best.'

'Thank you,' he offered, hangdog. 'Thank you, Mummy.'

'When shall I do it? Straightaway, as soon as I see him?'

'If you would. If you don't mind.' He hesitated, between cravenness and calculation. 'Get it over with, soon as he's home. That's in a couple of hours or less—? Oh Lord.' He mopped his forehead again. 'What I thought was, I'd come back at about half-past four and hang about—keep out of sight—till I see him go in. Then I give you, say . . . ten or fifteen minutes—?'

'Ten or fifteen!' she echoed hollowly. 'Give me a half-hour at least.'

'Half-hour it is. Well, that's that.' He rose, his usual aplomb conspicuous by its absence. 'Wish it could be now. This waiting, hell!—Poor old Mummy.' He smiled, miserably jocular. 'Not nice pushing you under the wheels, not nice at all. Just a hero, our Paul.' He turned to go, then checked abruptly. 'By the way, when I come back I shan't use my key, I—I'll ring. And *you* answer, please? One look at you and I'll know,' he stated with conviction, 'just how bad it's going to be. Maybe it'll do more harm than good, your taking the first wallop. But—but the sight of you would at least warn me to prepare—to brace myself—accordingly.'

'Yes,' she answered. 'All right.' As he disappeared into the hall she thought of something, and hurried after him. 'Paul, Paul!' Already at the door, he turned. 'Paul,' she urged. 'Don't ring more than once. He won't know it's you, he'd expect you to use your key. But if I don't answer straightaway—' she gulped, already short of breath with nervousness '—you'll know it's because—because—'

'—because you're in the middle of a rough passage,' he supplemented, unsmiling. 'O.K., I shan't ring twice—I'll wait.' The door closed behind him.

For a moment Mrs. Milland stood blankly, then like an automaton started to turn. Suddenly the silence and emptiness of the house came upon her; she stopped dead a moment before resuming her somnambulist's progress towards nothing better than the next half-hour that used her up with its mindless roamings here and there, its forays of thought— spasmodic, also useless. What use planning, actually; crises of this sort unfolded according to plan no more than a hurricane or other convulsion of nature . . .

Exhausted at last—*Stop thinking,* she commanded herself, *stop thinking.* At this rate she would be no more than a shapeless tatter of nerves, just when Paul had most need of her. *Let it come, then do what you can, if you can. . . .*

All at once it seemed to her that she would die if she could not lie down, close her eyes and let oblivion take her. Making for the sofa like a hunted animal she came up hard against some invisible barrier of shock, took a moment to recognize it as the doorbell, and thought *Go away, go away. Whoever you are, go away, away . . .* Yet by long automatic habit she moved cautiously to where, unseen, she could overlook the front steps, and peered out.

Her first shock was of unbelief, her second of headlong anger; she could not have thought that so much feeling survived in her cancellation. *What a trick of Paul's, what a wretched trick,* she fulminated silently, *sending her along like this without warning. Just when I can't take any more, I can't, I . . .* Abruptly she made a first movement of plunging again towards the sofa and paused as abruptly, knowing herself trapped. *She knows I'm here,* she reminded herself. *He's told her.* Perforce dragging herself to the door, she felt her outrage subside to a set hostility, not without a cruel sneering vein of definition: *Come to make her peace with the mother-in-law.*

Chantal's aspect and manner, Chantal's face especially,

might in the ordinary way have evoked her pity. With fear-haunted eyes enormous with question, her lips pulled out of shape by trembling, her whole body eloquent of her doubtful right to stand on this doorstep. . . .

'Madame,' she blurted at once in a shaken voice; she was holding hard to her courage, obviously. 'Excuse me, may I —please—speak with you a little—?'

What for? the other asked silently, but her curt, 'I expect so,' was off-putting enough to check the girl's first movement to enter.

'Not for long, I will not speak long,' she entreated, and the entreaty deepened, in Heather, her stoniness of rejection.

'Oh, come in,' she said brusquely, 'it's chilly,' with hard eyes watched the hesitant negotiation of the threshold, then closed the door smartly and turned on her prospective daughter-in-law. 'And it was a shabby trick of Paul's to send you along like this, on his heels, and not let me know in advance. Tell him that from me, will you.'

'Tell—?' Incomprehension made Chantal's immense eyes more immense. 'He has not sent me, madame, Paul has not sent me.'

'Oh, Lord!—'

'But I swear, *je vous le jure*,' Chantal countered the lash of scepticism and impatience. 'I have come of my own accord, Paul does not know, he knows nothing of it, he would be angry.' With renewed supplication she scanned Heather's face. 'He tell me not to come, he says Wait, wait till I speak with my father and mother. But I could not wait, I must come and speak to you, madame, I must.'

'Well,' said Heather after a moment, past belief or unbe-

186

lief in her profundity of disgust. 'Come in.' She led the way to the living-room. 'You'd better sit down,' she continued flatly, waited till Chantal had found a seat in slow motion, then seated herself and asked forbiddingly, 'Yes?'

'Madame,' Chantal began in a rush. 'I only wish—I have wished to tell you how—how it was when I have done you that *sale tour*, that dirty trick—how it was with me when I did it—'

'Oh Chantal, not again,' she repudiated. 'That's over and done with, I've told you—'

'But madame, please, please,' Chantal interrupted in turn. 'Never have I done somessing like ssiss to anyone, I must explain, I must tell you why. It is because I have been in love wiss Paul, so in love, but listen, listen.' She strained forward painfully. 'When he—when he has—wanted me at first—and I, I wanted him—but I was afraid, *j'étais viérge*, but all the same I—I say yes, I sleep wiss him—' she stumbled awkwardly '—then Paul he is *angry* wiss me because I am virgin, he say, Why didn't you tell me, he is angry!—Men,' she shrugged, her young voice heavy with ancient fatalism. 'But then he tell me, "well, the harm it is done, we may as well live near each other, it is better like that, more convenient. My mother wishes an au pair and I will get somebody to make you a recommendation, this is easy."—How he has done it I do not know,' she digressed. 'But you have accepted me and I come here and it is all right at first, and—and then—'

She stopped suddenly; her eyes looked back on pain.

'—and then it has become—*terrible*.' Her voice deepened tragically, yet even now was incredulous. 'For me, terrible. He sleeps wiss me, yes, but he goes away often, his parties, his weekends, and leaves me alone. If I am angry he laughs, he goes away all the same. He does what he wish, but what I wish—never once does it stop him, never!'

Again she had to halt to control her voice; Heather, developing a headache under this bombardment of Chantal's griefs and wrongs, also felt—against her will—a responsive aching in her throat.

'But he sleeps wiss me all the same, he uses me. I am his *joujou*, his *rien*.' A remniscent rage dried her incipient tears. 'Then I think, another girl, he has another girl where he goes for the weekend and leaves me sitting alone. Then I tell him he has someone else and he says Well, so what, we are not engaged to marry. Do not be jealous, it is stupid and boring. He stands there and yet he is not there, he is far away and I cannot—*reach* him, Oh madame, you do not know—!'

Don't I know, Chantal, silently she answered, out of a long fatigue. *Don't I know.*

'And then—and then—I am *enceinte*.' On this extinguishing disaster, again she was extinguished. 'And I tell him, and he . . . and he . . . '

Wonderingly her eyes searched the pattern so infinitely old, so shatteringly new to the one who faces it.

'—he says, Get rid of it at once, I will give you money. Then we fight like wolves, I tell him No, I will not, he is mine and yours, and he says, 'How do I know it is mine? Perhaps you have found someone else, you have plenty of time for it, I am away very much. He says this, madame, he *says* it!' Her fury crackled like a brush-fire. 'And I hit him, I—I—and after ssiss we are bad friends. But I love him all the same, I cannot stop loving him, I love him and I hate him. And even so, when he comes to my bed at night, I—

188

I *let* him!' It was a cry of raw outrage. 'And I think, what will become of the child, what will become of me, and I go mad. Madame, you are so calm, so *posée*, you will not understand, but I have gone crazy, crazy.'

Won't I understand, Mrs. Milland retorted again in silent antiphon, all at once seeing a picture of over thirty years ago, seeing and feeling it with scarifying vividness. This had been during a pre-engagement period when, dizzy with love for Ian and sometimes dizzy with despair, not yet sure of him, she had sat withdrawn into an alcove of a tennis club's lounge in Angmering, herself the only person there except for a woman sitting at the bar, a stranger to her and incidentally very pretty. Through the door and with utmost eagerness of gait there came, all at once, Ian. With the same eagerness, such as he had never shown towards her, he swooped on a stool next the woman and entered upon an intimate and animated exchange with her, every line of him, every inclination of body, expressing the assiduity and flattery of courtship. At the sight, the earth opened and dropped her into a void, a vacuum of ice-cold sickness from which she emerged a madwoman. *I'll kill him,* she thought coldly and deliberately, *I'll kill him,* and looked about for something to kill him with. Finding nothing she rose to her feet, moving outside herself, in the same lunatic trance approached the couple, still laughing and chatting in complete absorption with each other, and when she got nearer saw that the man was not Ian; a general resemblance and her own trifling short-sightedness had deceived her. But she would never forget the shock and lightning-bolt in her head, the transport of madness, literal icy madness.

'And if I go back to France like I was, *enceinte*, how

would it be for my family, *figurez-vous*, madame! Not my mother, no, she is divorced and married again, she would only be angry. But my grandmother and my great-aunt in Poitiers, they love me very much and I love them. They are old, they would be so sad, so ashamed, I will die sooner before I show my face to them. Because they are wonderful to me always, they are wonderful women.' Her voice shook with fervent entreaty. *'Des femmes vraiement remarquables,* madame, you do not know—'

But Heather knew; again she understood perfectly, being well enough acquainted with this type of provincial ancestress that she could almost see them; two small withered women, flat-chested, always wearing black; of sharp delicate features and thin silver hair worn in the style of fifty years ago; of a cold exquisite courtesy and reserve, of unobtrusive native distinction, and with all their fragility, somehow formidable. . . .

'At Mass they are the only ones to sit in the—the seats—apart,' Chantal was saying. 'Once there were *chanoines* but no more, so they sit in those places for the *chanoines.'*

A simultaneous vision of bold brassy Chantal trembling before two frail old beings, and of long rows of carved and canopied stalls for canons three centuries dead—all empty but for the two shrunken old ladies in black, enthroned there —would have touched her with hysterical amusement if the girl had given her time.

'So I am *folle.* I am sick and crazy wiss love and having a baby,' she pelted along, 'and thinking always, what will I do, what will I do. So I think, I will hurt somebody that Paul loves, I will hurt his mother, I will work badly and talk to her *les insolences,* I will dress like *une sauvage* so she is ashamed for me to go in and out of her house. Because I am miserable—and the misery in me, it turn to badness and ugliness—'

She broke off again, and out of Mrs. Milland's depletion towered a new incredulity, a transfixing of new, breathless rage. *If she dares!* she panted to herself incoherently. *If she dares—!* For, all too obviously, she was preparing to ask for the impossible—like all people, thought Heather, who have done something unforgivable and think that a little confession, a little cheap pathos, will make everything right. . . .

'So madame.' Chantal's eyes, riveted on her, were abject with supplication. 'So I—I wish to ask you, madame, to beg you—' She swallowed painfully. '—if you would not tell Paul about ssiss—ssiss ugly thing—I have done to you with Mr. McVeigh. Please if you would not tell him, please—!'

Heather relaxed; after all the girl was not petitioning for friendship, only for secrecy, and that much was in her power to give.

'I shan't,' she said briefly. 'I shan't tell Paul under any circumstances, and you can count on that entirely.'

'Because I—because I—' Hauntedly Chantal, against reassurance, laboured on. 'I am afraid. I think ssiss is the thing, the one thing—that would make him feel toward me—not good. I know ssiss, madame, I know it. Because for you he feel—he feel—' abruptly she cast off the trammels of English and launched herself on familiar waters. *'Il a pour vous un sentiment tout à fait different de ce qu'il nourrit pour tout autre person. Je crois vraiement qu'il vous adore, il—'*

'Yes,' Heather interrupted impatiently. 'It would do no good at all and might possibly do harm, I quite agree.'

'Thank you,' Chantal offered. 'Thank you, madame. Because he will not say how much he love you, it is not in his nature to say—to admit—but if he find out—'

'He won't find out, I've told you once,' a sharp voice cut through hers. 'You needn't go on and on about it.'

'Yes, yes, I . . .' Chantal was humble. She was beautiful too, astonishingly beautiful with her translucent look, the refined and purified look of recent illness, her eyes dark pools of supplication. 'I am sorry, madame, I am very sorry.' But now her air was less of a question settled than of preparation for something new—something not easily said. 'And you— you do not feel towards me good, you do not like me, and you are right. But now I am different, I will try to show you how different, I will try to deserve—'

'Don't try,' Heather interrupted savagely; the earlier suspicion, now confirmed, rekindled her to white heat. The girl *was* daring to ask for friendship after all; on top of everything else, she *dared* . . . Over Mrs. Milland broke, in flying spume and fury, a bitter sense of her ordeals past, present and to come. Her humiliation by Hugh, her consequent blasted ambitions and lowered dignity in her own home, the horror of the poisoning charge, the present prospect of breaking the news to Ian and taking the first shock of his rejection, in whatever form it came—and here was this creature, this stupid, young, selfish, beautiful creature, the one and only source of all the trouble, presuming to demand yet more of her, presuming to bid for the one thing it was not in her power to give. The insolence, unbearable . . . all of it surged up in Mrs. Milland and spilled over, boiling-hot and ice-cold, on the head that was to blame.

'Don't try to deserve friendship, if that's what you're talking about,' she railed in a voice like something tearing. 'Let's forget things like friendship and affection, they're beside the point. I'm not your enemy, and that's as much as you can hope for. In a little while I'll have to speak to Paul's father, tell him about this marriage, and how much do you think I like it, how do you think I—it's too much, too much, why must it be I, why must it always—' nearly toppling into self-pity and incoherence, by main force she held rigidly to her control. 'Well, it's all right, I'll do it for Paul, I'll do my best. And I wish you well in your marriage, I hope you'll make Paul happy, but don't ask me for more than that, because I've nothing more in me. Don't ask me to *feel!*' she berated like a fishwife. 'I'm tired, I'm tired, I've nothing to give. Not to you, not to the child, not anyone, anyone . . .'

As suddenly as she had begun she ran down; there was a considerable silence.

'Madame,' Chantal said finally. 'You are right. I know it, I have said already that you are right. I have said two bad lies, I have spoiled somessing and I am the loser. I shall pay for it all my life, I have begun paying now and it is right that I should pay. At night when one wakes up and the bad memories return, this is what will come back to me first of all.'

As she paused, curiously there came to Heather—still unstrung with resentment—an awareness of how perfect was her tone: composed and respectful but without petition, and this quality—this absence of petition—was strangely compelling.

'But one thing you have said—one thing only—is wrong.'

Was she hearing this bare-faced effrontery, or only imagining . . . ?

'You have said you have nothing to give me and nothing to give the child,' Chantal's voice came again through her unbelief. 'But how can you say ssiss? For whether you like it or not you have given me already, you have been kind to me, you only.' Gravely she regarded Heather. 'When you have come to my bedsit, to warn me—already you have been giving because you are defendng me. So ssiss child, you are defending him before he is born, because you have been defending his mother. So you see.' Her calm certitude of fact was as becoming to her as her air of humility had been unbecoming. 'I was stupid and bad and proud and I asked you for nothing. But you, *néanmoins*, you have given. Maybe you like it, maybe you do not like it. But all the same it is so. It is so and you cannot change it.'

Another silence followed, prolonged; to Mrs. Milland, somehow held in abeyance by the girl's serious look, there struggled dimly a still dimmer perception. You are presented willy-nilly with circumstances bearable or unbearable, out of which you must make your life. And you do, a surprised inner voice reminded her; you do. And the important thing somehow is with what grace you receive the good or endure the bad or indifferent; with what dignity . . . And to be stripped of compassion, was that in itself loss of dignity? it was something that had never occurred to her. Before she could reach for it, sudden fright plowed into her like an ice-breaker's steel beak.

'What time—' she gasped, sitting up suddenly '—what time is it?' and at Chantal's answer jumped up. 'Mr. Milland will be home at any moment, he mustn't find you here. Hurry, hurry! not the front door,' she gabbled. 'He might see you —the basement, quick. But make sure it's all clear first, make sure—!' The girl vanished like a shot and left her bound tight in a silence, listening . . . no alarums or excursions, her future daughter-in-law had obviously got away and why not, with the useful familiarity of ins and outs she had acquired in this house. . . .

Still angry and upset, she sat in the aftermath of the interview; her faint ironic tribute to Chantal's expertness overlaid with something else. Something strangely like relief, an easement of the heart deriving—incongruously—from what source? her memory of the girl's composed argument, the silent strength with which she had sustained the hail of recrimination and reproach? A strong character, she was compelled to admit, really strong . . . if only her grudging salute were not overshadowed with Ian's approach, and what she would have to tell him. And how, how; once again she was being shredded apart with knowledge of her inadequacy, the certitude that the manner of her communication would make a bad situation worse, would make it—in fact—hopeless. Too much depended on her and she was not up to it, her intractably-open nature knew no approach but the plain and direct. Fatal in this case, fatal past remedy. . . .

Through her tremor, with its stage-fright accompaniment of short breath and dry lips, the earlier thing touched her again with the curious moment of peace left in Chantal's wake; not enough to fortify her actually, not nearly enough, yet imparting its vague reassurance. If only she could think what it was, it might be something to hold onto . . . she groped for it, her ears tight and cracking as she listened for the front door, but had not yet captured it, up to the moment of hearing Ian's key in the lock.

XVI

He looked and sounded his usual self; elegant and composed. By endowment of nature his equilibrium, after domestic upheaval, seemed perfectly restored. Even his wife, enviously contrasting his immunity with her scars, had difficulty in deciding whether this perfection were entirely of the façade; whether something about him were not in some way altered, subtly darkened. The impression came and went, then she discovered that she loved his face especially when this unfamiliar grave look shadowed it; evanescent, perhaps imagined . . . ?

She watched him pour drinks as usual and approach her, delicately holding the stem of her sherry glass with three fingers—he had excellent hands, fine and shapely—watched him set down the brimming glass without spilling a drop, and watched him turn and start walking towards his own chair. With ludicrous comminglement of major crisis with domestic insignificance she reflected that the coming scene would benefit little by the addition of spilled whisky or even broken glass, and waited till he had placed his own drink with similar precision.

'Ian,' she blurted, before he had time to settle comfortably. She had had enough of terrorstricken peerings for the right moment; there was no right moment. 'Ian, I've got to tell you that Paul and Chantal are marrying.'

Only just seated and about to lean back he stopped dead, remaining forward in the chair and looking at her without expression; after a moment he said evenly, 'If this is a joke, I don't find it amusing.'

'Not a joke,' she returned. 'They're marrying tomorrow. He was here awhile ago and told me.'

'Told *you*,' he echoed after a moment. 'So you could break it to daddy, eh? Hadn't the guts to tell me himself, no. Told you.'

'I couldn't—help—' in her hollow fear was a hollow relief; at least it was out. 'It's no pleasure to me, what he asked me to—'

'Marrying that . . .' his unhearing voice cut her off. '. . . that cheap little whore, that lying dirty layabout's convenience . . .' He stood up suddenly. 'I won't have it. I won't have it, do you hear?'

'Ian,' she protested. 'He came and told me. He wasn't asking my permission, he wasn't asking yours, he was *telling* me—'

'And you let him?' he demanded. 'You sat there and—and accepted this monstrosity, simply—simply let—what ailed you?' he assailed her. 'Why couldn't you get him to wait—persuade, beg, anything—till I'd a chance to speak with him?—'

'It wouldn't have done any good,' she countered no less

197

loudly than he, emboldened by despair. 'He was perfectly sure of himself and perfectly determined. You'd have done nothing but make a horrible scene, you'd have got nowhere with him—'

'How do you know I'd have got nowhere?' he bayed. 'What do you know about it, what have you ever known about it? I can do anything I want with him without his realizing, I've always been able to do it. And you too stupid to know it, too woolly-minded, God!—What do you amount to, what're you good for?' he flung at her. 'Nothing but to make trouble —messes—that somebody else has to pull you out of. My God, your stupidity, your feeble, ruinous stupidity—!'

Throttled by multiple angers he stopped all at once, his breathing audible in the dead silence. His wife made no immediate effort to reply, being preoccupied merely with endurance of his contempt, the need to shield herself with what rags of dignity she might, and with facing the stark final impact, the end of all civilization between them. It was another of those matrimonial moments of truth like their clash after the poisoning charge, only a thousand times worse; a moment when the buried accumulation of years starts from its grave all at once and the last decent shroud is torn from the body of naked insult. Pale and rigid, empty of retort for the moment, she saw her husband transformed once more by the malignance in his face that prophesied the coming old man, unrecognizable. . . .

'Ian,' she said at last, with uttermost care. Her voice was as dry of timbre as her mind of resource. *You're wrong about Chantal* had nearly escaped her; she shied away from it, as though she had nearly dropped a live coal among bone-dry leaves in a wood. 'All right, I . . . didn't manage it very well,

but—but there seemed to me no—no question of management.'
Pausing on an access of fatigue, once more there came to
her that distant clearing of some horizon always about to be
seen but not seen, not yet, not yet . . . 'But I—I implore you
to be careful, terribly careful.'

'What more did he tell you?' he extorted as if unhearing.
'What else—?'

'He said he had lied from beginning to end about Chantal.'
She snatched the opportunity she could not have expected.
'And if she lied about him, out of revenge, he said he'd
more or less driven her to it. He said he'd behaved badly and
she'd behaved badly and they both wanted to—to—'

Something stopped her suddenly, an imminence like warning.

'—to make it up to each other—'

And the enlightenment that had delayed in its hinterland
came up strong all at once, overpowering, and with it the
identity of the other thing—the release—she had felt before
she recognized it. What she had seen and not known she
had seen was the sight of two young people rising up from
the destruction of the lie, breaking free of the stake in the
ground and its crippling tether, and the sight had simply
brought her to life again. Her appeasing servitude fell away
from her as though it never had been; her neck, aching under
the yoke, rose free.

'Ought to be done in cheap stained glass,' a voice invaded
her altitudes; Ian was enviably unaware that before him
was a different creature. 'Or an inspirational calendar.—
Where is he? somewhere behind your skirts?'

'He's coming later,' she returned neutrally.

'When?'

'He didn't say,' she evaded, reminding herself that it was only her unimportant coil that was unknotted, and that Paul's had yet to be.

'Well.' Ian dug his hands into his pockets and stared before him. 'Have to think of something.'

His inflection, no less than his words, roused her to renewed and different watchfulness; she waited.

'Think of something quickly, in the time we've got—you've no idea how much—?'

She shook her head.

'Have to find . . . something . . .' he pursued in that voice of cogitation. 'She's been clever enough to get round him. Well.' He brooded for another moment. 'If I can't be at least as clever as that little slut, it's too bad.'

'I don't expect abusing her to him will do any good,' she offered briefly.

'Neither do I.' He had taken her warning for cooperation. 'I wasn't putting my faith in abuse, we'd need something more . . . substantial.'

We: a confirming qualm touched her at that *we*, and his assumptions that it signalled.

'A damned sight more substantial,' he mused. An air of good humour was suffusing him by degrees, a smile of baleful appetite. 'And just possibly we have it.'

'What?' she asked, in a chill of knowing before she knew.

'Well.' He smiled even more broadly. 'All this nobility you describe, this mutual exoneration, may have included mutual confession.' He rocked a little on his heels. 'Full mutual confession possibly, or possibly not full. We'll see —we'll see.'

'What do you mean?' she asked a little shrilly.

'I mean whether, in her little pose of purification and re-vealing all, our Chantal may not, in a tactful way, have suppressed one or two small details.' He was licking his lips spiritually, if not physically. 'Such as the trick she played you with Hugh. Eavesdropping over the phone? Selling her information? Moderately nasty, eh?' he smiled with eye-lids half-drooping. 'Paul's sentimental over you, you know, decidedly soppy. Not a nice picture of his future wife, eh?' His drowsy look tucked her in with him, cozily, beneath the blankets of complicity. 'Likely to tarnish the image a bit—?'

'You aren't going to tell him that!' she blurted, for all her imagined preparedness aghast. 'You'd never—!'

'No?' His smile deepened very slightly. 'No?'

'But—but—' she strove incoherently '—a thing like that —when they've already so much to—to live down between them—make up and forget—and this with everything else they've got against them, this one thing more might—might weigh the balance against them, hopelessly—' she snatched a breath '—Ian, you can't do it! you can't!'

'Can't I?' he queried dulcetly. 'Can't I?'

'No! no!'

'Again?' he cut off her clamour. 'You're putting in your oar again? Christ, it's beyond belief.—Now listen to me.' His tone fell dangerously low. 'Keep out of this. I'm warning you, keep out of it. Don't you see, you fool—'

A vacuum of incredulity rang in her ears at the limitless hatred in his voice; what she had thought the worst between them, so far, had been by no means the worst.

'Don't you see,' the deadly serration ground on against her, 'it's the only chance of pulling him free of this—this muck? One word from you, one word out of turn when I'm telling him and—damn you, I'll strangle you. This is the one card I've got to play, the one strong card, and by God I'll play it.'

'If you do,' she said without emotion, 'I'll leave you.'

During a silence her words came back to her, their content worlds apart from the identical mutual threat of their earlier quarrel, the untenable position that neither of them could abandon quickly enough. These words she meant, they had fallen like a descending axe, nor could she have weighted them so lethally without her new certitude—her freedom that was the gift of Paul and Chantal.

'I won't stop in the same house with you one moment longer than I can help,' she went on in the same level voice. 'Not with a man who could do such a thing. I'll go out charring first.'

He stared at her, blank with malevolence.

'And if you do what you say,' she pursued, 'you may spoil things for them—prevent the marriage—but you'll lose Paul.'

He believed her; she saw it. Still staring, he made no answer at all. After a moment his eyes went empty and fell away from hers, seeming to grope in the corners of the room; at the same time an effacement passed over him, a sort of dulling. After another moment he sat down, beaten. And surmounting her perception of this beaten look was something she was not ashamed to acknowledge as triumph, and vengeful triumph. The half-starved years of her marriage, when she had wasted herself in love and longing and abject blame for some poverty in herself, some lack . . . and at last, and after all, to be exonerated. Not a lack in herself, but an emptiness in him. *He doesn't like to love*, she thought. *He likes to hate*. This was the mystery she had been unable to plumb, the secret key she had been unable to find: that there was no key. Even his love for Paul, or what she had taken for his love, was it rather the sense of Paul as *his,* his possession that had to talk, think and exist by his father's standards? Likely; more than likely. *Poor Ian,* she thought for the first time in her life, *poor Ian.* A conclusive peace filled her, the serenity of arrival, and with it began a bubbling-up, an effervescence of bright images long abandoned: colours and light, her hands with brushes in them; Paris, work in a studio; Robbie. And no one to hinder her now, no one to impede . . .

She glanced at him and in the same moment found, as it happened, that he was looking at her. And he sensed the liberation in her glance, and at once was uneasy under it.

'What are you smirking at?' he asked gently and venomously. 'Like the village idiot, if one may say so?'

'Nothing,' she returned. Her tranquil voice, instead of appeasing, discounted him, and he knew it. For a moment he sat silent with a darkening in his face, then began to say something; the doorbell, a single brief ring, cut him off.

'Oh Christ,' he said viciously. 'Now, of all . . . Take care of it, d'you mind?'

Caught equally between the counter-forces of automatic compliance on one side, and her private knowledge on the other, for an instant she sat paralyzed.

'Go ahead, do,' he was urging irritably. 'Unless—were you expecting someone?'

'No,' she denied, scared witless again by habit and by emergency.

'Well then, get rid of—anyway, at this time of day, who'd it be—?'

'It's Paul,' she admitted, driven to the wall, and saw him surge upright from his chair in a single convulsive movement and then, all at once, stand still. His face was stricken with furies cancelling each other out: fury of hatred and impotent anger, fury of knowing he had just suffered a major defeat at the hands of his wife and was about to suffer another at the hands of his son, with the only alternative to that defeat another defeat of loss, and permanent loss.

For once in his life he's got to knuckle under, flashed through her with vengeful pleasure. *Not easy for him, he's had no training for it,* then saw something not visible to her before. His metallic rigidity was not rigidity; a pulsation shook him almost imperceptibly, a faint continuous tremor that seemed to blur his outlines. . . .

And to Mrs. Milland the sight, all at once, was unendurable. With bitterest shame for her gloating of a moment ago she saw her husband's self-esteem in ruins at his feet, his dear vanity and what else had he, what else has anyone when it comes to it . . . Moving outside herself and without previous intention she went to him, flung her arms about him, and at once felt his whole body stiffen with his first impulse to thrust her away. Yet the thrust, from his inmost core, somehow failed on the edge of accomplishment; he let her go on clinging to him, a frozen image in the living encirclement.

'Ian,' she breathed. 'Ian, Ian.'

We'll lose him, she was going to say again. *If you make things impossible we'll lose him, he'll be through with us,* then in the same instant recoiled from duress of warnings that could only hammer home his subjugation.

'Ian,' she began again. 'He loves you, he admires you so much, he's so terrified of being on—on bad terms with you,

so afraid that—that you won't forgive him, or—or have anything more to do with him—'

With all the ardour of entreaty she kissed his lips, felt
their inimical deadness beneath her own, and hurried on
because she dared not stop.

'And the girl, she's utterly—respectable—' a suppressed
hysteria of amusement rent her at the word: *her grandmother
and great-aunt sit in the canons' stalls at Mass,* all but escaping her, nearly toppled her into wild laughter. 'Paul lied to
you about her, he admits he lied,' she babbled on. 'Give them
a chance, please—!' She was failing, she was on the brink of
seeing her whole family life break up and disappear, and
cast about her for a working spell of words like a drowning
swimmer for handholds. Her own desires and hopes were
the least of it, they had waited so long, let them wait a little
longer. In this moment nothing was clear to her but the need
to save her husband from humiliation; at all costs it was right,
it was worth it, that she should throw all of herself into the
discard for the sake of upholding her husband's dignity.

'Ian!' she was supplicating meanwhile. 'With Hugh that
time—and when Paul was accused—you were strong and I
was nothing, I was good for nothing, you were strong for
both of us. Now for both of us, Ian, be kind. Please, darling,
please, for both of us!—be kind to them!—'

She kissed him again, a kiss of petition yet a lover's kiss,
and hardly dared believe she felt under it not response, yet
a faintest acceptance. Still holding him, fearfully she withdrew her lips from his and ventured to look at him, finding
a face of unqualified grimness, yet recognizably Ian's; not
the face of that other one, the old withered malevolence,
coming.

'He hasn't rung again,' he said all at once, disconcertingly and with contemptuous amusement. 'You and he arranged this, didn't you? He was to stop outside till Mummy'd made weather-signals?'

Still clinging hard, she saw him being restored, his male ascendancy coming together intact, and wholeheartedly made to him a concession whose blind instinct forever towered above clearest-eyed logic. Concession was her loss, contention perhaps her victory—her lonely victory, bitter and barren as ashes.

'That's how?' he mocked her hesitation, drawing his advantage—as always—from her disadvantage. And if by her love she had cherished and established this pattern, yet it was beyond her to regret having loved.

'That's how you laid it on?' he was gibing. 'You and your heroic son?'

'Yes,' she admitted, offering him by her shamed face and deprecating voice the necessary victor's laurel. Withdrawing her arms from what had felt inhuman as steel and now felt like a body, she went to open the door.